CRESCENT CITY WOLF PACK

5

A SONG TO REMEMBER

CARRIE PULKINEN

A Song to Remember

Contact Information: www.CarriePulkinen.com

Edited by Victoria Miller

ISBN: 978-1-7347624-2-6

CHAPTER ONE

SHANE ANDERSON CLUTCHED THE STEERING wheel and peeled out of the hotel parking lot, merging onto the highway and narrowly avoiding a collision with a pickup truck. He jerked the wheel right, and the rumble of reflectors beneath his tires reminded him to focus on the road.

What have those bloody witches done this time?

Ricardo's voice over the phone had sounded frantic. He'd mumbled something about Cammie botching a spell to release Shane from their idiotic plan and passing out. They needed him there to complete the incantation and keep Cammie from slipping into a magic-induced coma.

Something was off, though, and skepticism

clawed through his chest, his wolf growling a warning in his mind. If this was some kind of joke or their way of getting even after he'd left the band…

"Bloody hell." He'd met his fate-bound tonight. Witches couldn't fathom the connection a werewolf felt when he met his soulmate. They probably thought they were being funny, dragging him out of bed and away from the woman he was meant to spend the rest of his life with.

But if Cammie really was hurt, he had to help her. He'd do whatever he needed to and be done with the witches for good. Then he'd get his ass back to Bekah and convince her the night they'd shared was the beginning of forever.

He'd pack his bags and move to New Orleans tomorrow. Hell, he'd follow his fate-bound anywhere; his wolf wouldn't have it any other way.

Pulling into the apartment parking lot, he cut the engine and ran his hand across the worn leather of his saxophone case in the passenger seat. The brass name-plate felt cool against his fingers, and the engraving of his name had smoothed so much it barely registered on his skin.

Looking into Bekah's eyes tonight, every broken piece of his world converged, snapping back together.

Her presence filled in the blank spots, making him whole, and it all made sense now. Leaving his home in London, his dad disowning him so he couldn't go back, following a doomed relationship on a tour of the United States, being dumped in Florida...it all led him to today.

To his fate-bound.

He drummed his fingers on the sax case. New Orleans was the perfect place for him to settle down and open his music school. At least his mum would've been proud of him if she were still here.

A balmy Florida breeze mussed his hair as he climbed out of his Jeep and slammed the door. He hit the lock button on his key fob and jogged across the parking lot to Ricardo's apartment. As he lifted his hand to knock, the door swung open and Ricardo ushered him inside.

A dozen black candles illuminated the room in flickering firelight, and the overwhelming aroma of incense and herbs assaulted his nose, stinging his eyes. The furniture had been pushed against the walls, and a pentagram drawn in white powder took up most of the living room floor.

Shane's heart thrummed, his wolf's warning growl growing louder in his mind. "What the hell is going on, mate? Where's Cammie?"

Regret flashed in Ricardo's eyes. "I'm sorry, buddy. If you're not with us, you're a liability."

Cammie stepped into the room wearing a black, hooded robe. The moment she lifted her arms toward Shane, a wall of magic slammed into him, knocking the breath from his lungs. He called on his wolf, his fight instinct kicking into high gear, and his body hummed with magic as he shifted form.

Ears flat against his head, he bared his teeth and growled, cutting his gaze between Ricardo and Cammie.

Ricardo squealed and jumped over the couch. "You said he wouldn't be able to shift, Cam. Change him back."

"Give me a second." She fisted her hands and then splayed her fingers, sending another blast of dark magic toward Shane, neutralizing his own.

A quivering sensation ran through his entire body as he lost hold of his wolf and transformed to human.

"What are you doing?" Panic surged, a thrumming, vibrating urgency turning his blood to liquid fire. He tried to run, but his muscles seized, the room pressing down on him, the unbearable heaviness bringing him to his knees.

Cammie's eyes rolled back as a string of Latin

words flowed from her blood-red lips, and dark magic pricked at Shane's skin, clawing at the base of his skull. He tried to stand, to get the hell out of there, but his body betrayed him. He was paralyzed, the pressure and pain making his stomach churn and his vision swim.

Ricardo clutched his wrist, holding it against his chest as he dragged a cursed blade across Shane's forearm. Searing pain exploded across his skin, and blood dripped into a bowl before his were magic sealed the wound.

His wolf howled in his head, but Shane didn't need to be reminded of the consequences. Were blood held powerful magic that no witch should ever have access to. He tried to speak, but his jaw clenched tight, his teeth grinding together until sharp pain shot through his temple.

Ricardo shoved him to the floor, and he landed on his side, his cheek pressing into the rough carpet. Cammie stopped chanting, and the pressure lifted, but his body felt like a lump of rock.

She knelt to run her fingers through Shane's hair. "It would be easier to kill him. We have his blood. That's all we need."

"He's our friend, Cam. I can't have that on my conscience." Ricardo set the bowl on a table. "Just wipe his mind, and we'll dump him down the road like we agreed."

Shane groaned, trying to force words through his thickening throat, but they wouldn't come. The witches were the closest he had to family, and sadly, their betrayal was far from surprising.

"Roll him onto his back." Cammie dipped a spoon into the bowl of blood and added a single drop to a glass of purple liquid. As soon as the drop hit the surface, the mixture flashed bright pink and steam rose from the container. "He's got to swallow this for the spell to work."

Ricardo shoved his shoulder, and his muscles screamed as he rolled to his back. "Our plans require a blood sacrifice from everyone involved. You were already in it, so you can't back out." He patted his shoulder. "Don't worry man, in a few minutes, you won't remember anything."

With his thumb on Shane's chin, Ricardo pried his lips apart and poured the steaming mixture into his mouth. The sickly-sweet liquid burned his tongue and the back of his throat, but he refused to swallow. These witches would not steal his memory, nor would he play a role in their black magic scheme. This paralyzing spell would wear off eventually, and then they'd pay.

Ricardo looked at Cammie. "He's not swallowing."

The witch let out a dramatic sigh and bent over Shane, pinching his nose so he couldn't breathe. He tried to shake his head, to curl his hands into fists, to move *anything* on his body, but he was frozen. His lungs ached for air, pressure building in his chest like a stack of cinder blocks sat atop him.

Instinct took over, and he gasped for breath, sucking the magic concoction down his throat. He choked, sputtering the liquid and inhaling it again as a coughing fit wracked his body. The potion singed his sinuses, scorching from the back of his throat up to his watering eyes. Ricardo rolled him onto his side, and purple splattered across the floor as he expelled the last of the contents from his throat.

"He didn't swallow it all." Ricardo hauled him up, and his legs wobbled as the paralyzing spell began to lose its hold.

"He got enough," Cammie said. "Put him in his car and drive. I'll follow you."

His vision tunneled into darkness, and he squeezed his eyes shut. When he opened them, a woman in a black robe lowered her hood to reveal long, blonde hair. Where had she come from?

She looked familiar, and he wracked his brain, but her name eluded him. "Who are you?"

The woman smiled. "It's already working. Let's dump him before he gets all his strength back. Take his phone and wallet. We don't want him finding us later."

The man emptied his pockets and dragged him out the door. Shane tried to pull from his grasp, but he stumbled, and the man shoved him into the back seat of a car. His muscles ached, and his head spun as they sped down the highway. On a secluded section of road, the driver pulled over and hauled him out of the back seat, settling him behind the wheel.

He took in the man's dark hair and eyes, and familiarity pricked in his mind. "I know you, don't I?"

"Not anymore." The man slammed the door and jogged toward a van.

He watched as the van disappeared down the road, and he ran his hands over the leather steering wheel in front of him. He'd gotten in this car for a reason, but he couldn't recall what it was. He was going…somewhere. He needed to see someone, but…

Panic surged ice-cold through his veins. A million thoughts danced around the outskirts of his memory, swirling in a tornado of muddled perplexity, but he couldn't grab onto any of them. He didn't know where he was nor where he was going. *Bloody hell.* He didn't even know *who* he was.

New Orleans.

Through the jumbled, incomprehensible blankness of his mind, that one name was a lighthouse in the fog. A beacon of hope. Whatever happened to his memory, he would find it in New Orleans.

CHAPTER TWO

NINE HOURS EARLIER

"In what universe is summoning a demon ever a good idea?" Shane sat his saxophone case on the floor and clenched his fists at his sides, sucking in a gulp of air. The mere mention of getting help from a fiend raised his hackles, and his wolf hovered dangerously near the surface.

Ricardo was insane. That was the only explanation.

"It's not *a* demon. We're making a deal with Amdusias. He's a duke of hell, and he rules over music." Ricardo palmed his shoulder. "He can make our dreams come true."

"*Your* dreams." Shane shrugged off the witch's hand and marched toward Cammie, who sat with her legs curled beneath her on a brown sofa. "Are you in on this too?"

The blue-eyed witch twirled a drumstick in her fingers and blew a pale-pink bubble the size of her face. The gum popped, and she worked it back into her mouth before answering. "We're *all* in on this. The initial connection has been made. We have to finish the ritual beneath the full moon tomorrow night, and fame and fortune will be ours." Her bright-red lips curved into a smile, and she tucked a blonde curl behind her ear. "Relax, wolfman. We aren't going to summon him into the flesh. We'll bring him close enough to the surface for his energy to pass into us, and then we'll shut the gates."

The gates. The witches were planning to open the gates of hell as casually as a barn door…and they didn't see the problem with it.

"How did you make the initial connection? How are we *all* in this already?"

Cammie glanced toward Ricardo and lifted one shoulder. "It was just a bit of hair. Ricardo picked it up from the floor when you guys had your little bro date and got your hair cut together."

"You took my hair?" He glared at the lead singer.

Ricardo raised his hands. "It was going in the trash anyway."

"You're part of this, Shane." Cammie smiled and popped her gum.

"Jesus Christ." Raking a hand through his hair, he glared at his other bandmates. "You'll sell your souls for a chance at success?"

"Souls are overrated." Ricardo laughed. "Anyway, man, we're not going to promise our souls. We're going to give him our lives right now, let Amdusias run our careers. He'll be our manager. Cammie's agreed to let him speak to her through her dreams."

Shane took another deep breath and focused on the twenty-by-thirty landscape painting hanging above Cammie's head. Snow clung to the ground and trees in the image, a far cry from the humid Florida weather he'd gotten used to. He hadn't seen a white Christmas in five years, and if he had his way, he never would again.

The kind of success his friends wanted would require touring. A different city every night. Different weather. No stability. He'd been there, done that, and experienced the fall-out when things didn't work out.

"You're all crazy. You know that?" Any Witch Way consisted of five members: four American witches and Shane, the token werewolf. The only Brit. While his friends' musical ability was decent enough to land gigs at weddings, small venues, and hotel bars, like the one they were about to play, they would never achieve stardom with their mediocre talent.

Shane was counting on that.

"C'mon, dude. You're the only one of us who's had a taste of fame, and we want to sample that deliciously sweet stardom too," Ricardo said.

"And that went swimmingly for me, didn't it?"

"You could have moved back to jolly old London, mate," Ricardo mocked Shane's accent, "but you stayed. Don't tell me you wouldn't do anything to get that back."

"I won't sell my soul." There was no use arguing with them. All creative types had egos, and convincing them stardom wasn't all they imagined it would be was impossible. He'd been in their position once. The lure of fame was hard to ignore.

Of course, he'd been more interested in the woman that came with the package. Being in a famous rock band was never his dream; it just happened to be part of the deal.

But that was over now.

"I want out. I'll play tonight's show, and then I'm done."

"We need you, Shane." Cammie rose to her feet. "You're the most talented member of the band, and your songs are killer."

"No one wants to hear original music at the gigs we've been booking," Ricardo said. "If we don't do this, we'll be stuck playing crappy covers to small crowds who are more interested in getting drunk than hearing good music. It's time to expand our horizons."

Shane tried to hold back his groan, but it came out as a heavy sigh. "I get it, okay? I really do." And while he didn't share his mates' desire to make the band any bigger than it was, he didn't want to hold his friends back. "But asking a demon for help will only lead to trouble. Black magic is nothing to play with."

Cammie scoffed. "As if a werewolf knows more about magic than a witch."

He gritted his teeth. "I know plenty about demons." In London, the werewolves acted as the supernatural police force of the city. They were the demons' sworn enemies. Their job was to keep London safe from the fiends and the idiots who summoned them.

"My dad taught me all I need to know, but..." Cammie cut her gaze to Ricardo again, a silent agreement passing between them. "If you want out, we'll let you out. Finish the gig tonight. Sleep on it, and if you're still not convinced in the morning, you're free.

You just have to promise not to spill our secret when we become famous."

Cammie clutched Ricardo's bicep, resting her other hand on his shoulder before kissing him on the cheek. They were a perfectly matched couple now, but being in the spotlight tended to tear people apart.

"Think about it, old friend." Ricardo squeezed his shoulder. "That's all we ask."

Shane didn't have to think about it. Communing with demons went against his very nature. If he were a pack member, he'd be obliged to report the witches' intended activity to the alpha. Being rogue, he answered to no one, but he'd be damned if he'd let them turn a demon loose on Pensacola.

"All right, mate. I can give you that much." He'd let them think he was considering their scheme, anyway. "But for the record, I happen to enjoy the crappy covers. People appreciate familiarity."

"And when our album goes platinum, bands will be doing covers of our stuff. We'll be the familiar ones." Cammie clutched her drumsticks and strutted toward the door. "The stage is waiting, boys."

Shane picked up his sax case and slung his guitar over his shoulder. This was what he got for joining a band of witches.

Bekah Beauchamp stopped at the hotel bar and ordered a glass of rosé. Sectioned off from the restaurant, the spacious bar had elegant, modern lighting. Multiple nooks with tables and deep-blue upholstered chairs surrounded a small dance floor where a band had set up their instruments on the adjacent stage.

She sipped her wine, savoring the way the blend managed to be fruity and slightly dry at the same time, and scanned the crowd for her new friend. Tambra, a witch she'd met at the restauranteur conference in Pensacola, had convinced her to listen to the band playing in the bar on the last night of the symposium.

Her first instinct had been to decline the invitation. She needed to organize her notes from the day, plus she planned to drive home to New Orleans first thing in the morning. She hadn't seen Emma in three days, and though she'd spoken to her daughter on the phone every night at bedtime, a constant ache had formed in her chest from missing the little squirt.

Emma was in good hands with her grandma, though, and it wasn't like Bekah could make the drive home safely tonight. Still, a pang of guilt flashed through her chest every time she sipped her drink.

"Bekah!" Tambra waved, and six gold bangle bracelets slid up to her elbow. A matching gold flower hairpin adorned her short, blonde curls, and dark-gray, shimmery shadow created a smoky effect around her blue eyes.

A knot released in Bekah's chest as she strode toward the table Tambra had claimed on the edge of the dance floor. Though her own makeup was a far cry from the smoky-eyed vixen look of Tambra's palette, Bekah had applied a little extra shadow and a darker-than-normal shade of lipstick. But her attempt at making herself feel alive again had gifted her with a weighty dose of self-consciousness instead.

"Hey, Tambra. Thanks for inviting me." Bekah slid into the seat next to the witch.

"Thank you for coming. My cousin, Cammie, is the drummer, and she'd kill me if she knew I was in town and didn't see her show." She clinked her glass to Bekah's. "A woman sitting alone in a bar always attracts the weirdos who assume she's looking for a date. You saved me from deflecting all the beer-breathed come-ons tonight."

Bekah laughed. "It's been so long since I've had a night out, I wouldn't recognize a come-on if the beer breath stared me in the face." Nor would she know how to react. She hadn't attempted to flirt with anyone since the day she found out she was pregnant with Emma.

"A beautiful, successful woman like you? C'mon, you've probably got all your male packmates falling over themselves to get to you." Tambra lifted the chardonnay to her lips.

Drumming her nails on the table, Bekah shook her head. "I haven't had a date in eight years."

Tambra choked, sputtering wine across the table. "Girl." She swiped the cocktail napkin on the surface, absorbing the mess. "Eight years?"

"Not since Emma's dad left." She shrugged. "I'm a single mom. Most men tuck tail and run as soon as they find that out."

"Even werewolves? The men seem like such protectors."

"Especially werewolves. Emma's father is a witch, so we won't know if she'll be a shifting wolf or have witch powers until she comes into her magic. Only first-born weres can shift, so if Emma has that ability, whatever mate I ended up with wouldn't have shifting offspring of his own. No one wants to take that chance."

Tambra's brow furrowed. "Werewolves are assholes."

Bekah laughed. "So are witches."

"Isn't everyone? Well, if werewolves are out, you can still date humans, can't you?"

"I could, but I've been so busy between raising Emma, finishing college, and then opening my café. I haven't thought about it much." She traced her fingers across the wood pattern on the table. That was a lie. She *had* thought about it. Taking care of an eight-year-old on her own, she rarely got a moment alone, but lately, she'd never felt lonelier.

Tambra waved the waiter over and ordered another round of wine. "Maybe it's time you started."

"Maybe it is. I feel guilty though. I mean, I'm a mom first, and Emma…"

The witch held up a finger. "You're a woman first, and your daughter would benefit from seeing her mother happy and modeling healthy relationships."

She opened her mouth to argue, but she couldn't form a rebuttal. "Jeez, Tambra, forget restaurants. You should go into therapy."

"Ten years as a bartender, and you learn how to talk to people about their problems." She held up her glass in a toast. "To your first night out and the start of finding Bekah, the woman, again. She's in there somewhere."

"I'll drink to that." Bekah sipped her rosé, and a weight lifted from her shoulders. Tambra was right;

she was a woman first, and she'd lost herself along the way.

Things were different now, though. Emma was in school and wise beyond her years. Bekah was done with college, and her café was running smoothly. She had a bit of free time, a luxury she could never afford before. Maybe she should focus some of her energy on herself for a change. It was time she found the woman she'd lost, and she would start by letting go of her mom guilt and enjoying herself tonight.

A side door opened, and the band shuffled through. Tambra waved and shouted, "Cammie," and a young woman with long blonde hair and bright-red lips waved, her eyes lighting up with her smile.

Drumsticks in hand, Cammie trotted toward their table and hugged Tambra. "I'm so glad you came."

"I wouldn't miss my baby cousin's show. I even brought a friend. This is Bekah."

"Hi." Bekah shook Cammie's hand, and the witch's magical signature shimmied up her arm along with her emotions. Wiping her palm on her jeans, Bekah tried to keep her expression neutral. She'd learned to control her empathic ability as a teen, and she rarely picked up on anyone's feelings unless she wanted to.

But Cammie's emotions undulated through her, their intensity making them impossible to ignore. The natural excitement and anticipation for her upcoming performance paled in comparison to another type of eagerness spiked with fear.

"Nice to meet you." Cammie turned to Tambra. "Will you be around after the show?"

"You know it." Tambra smiled fondly as Cammie mounted the stage and settled behind the drum set.

Bekah shivered as the last of Cammie's emotions dissipated from her consciousness. "Is she okay? She seems a little…nervous."

"Oh, she's fine." Tambra waved off her concern. "She's always been high-strung."

"She must've been a handful as a kid."

As the rest of the band members set up their instruments, Bekah's gaze locked on a tall, dark-haired man beside the keyboard. He set a black acoustic guitar on a stand and knelt to open an instrument case.

"Who is that?" Bekah pointed at the tall drink of water and knocked her empty wine glass over on the table. She caught it before it could roll off the edge, but she made enough of a commotion to capture the handsome musician's attention.

He glanced up from his case and looked at her

with the most piercing set of sea-green eyes she'd ever seen. A short, dark beard accentuated his strong jaw, and as one corner of his mouth tugged into a crooked grin, her heart lost count of its rhythm.

"Close your mouth, hon, you're gaping at the man." Tambra snatched the empty glass from her hand and set it on the table behind them. "That's Shane."

Bekah snapped her mouth shut and leaned back in her chair, reminding herself to breathe. If a simple smile from a stranger could send her pulse racing like this, she definitely needed to get out more.

Shane pulled a saxophone from the case and set it on another stand next to the guitar. As he attached the mouthpiece, he flicked his gaze to Bekah again and nodded a hello.

Dammit, she was still staring at him. Biting her lip, she lifted her fingers in a pathetic attempt at a wave and shifted in her chair to face Tambra. "What...umm...What does he play?"

Tambra grinned. "Everything. Keyboard, guitar, sax. He's good with his hands and his mouth, if that's what you're wondering."

Her laugh came out as a snort, and she covered her mouth. "I was not wondering that."

"If a guy like Shane looked at me the way he's

been looking at you, that's exactly what I'd be wondering." She nudged her with an elbow. "I'm pretty sure he's single too."

Her body warmed, and though she was tempted to fan herself with a napkin, she refrained. Instead, she took a few slow, deep breaths to calm the raging hormones that had finally broken the dam.

The band opened the set with an Imagine Dragons cover, and Shane's fingers flew across the keyboard so effortlessly he could have played it with his eyes closed. At times he did, and when he opened them again, he glanced at Bekah, almost as if to be sure she was watching.

As the set went on, Tambra ordered another glass of wine, but Bekah had no need for alcohol. The way her body reacted to watching the sexy musician was better than any buzz the wine could have provided.

"What else do you know about Shane?" She glanced at Tambra before focusing on the man.

"Well…he's a werewolf, but don't let that discourage you. He's the most mature one of the bunch."

Her heart sank. She'd suspected as much based on his looks and the confident way he carried himself, but the only way to truly know a magical being's nature was through touch. The buzzing, electrical signature emanating from their skin was like a super-natural calling card.

Oh, well. Better to find out now so she could temper the hormones surging through her core. Shane was nice to look at, but that's all he could be, which was fine. At least she knew she could still be attracted to a man.

As the set ended, Tambra jumped from her seat and sashayed to the stage to talk to her cousin, leaving Bekah alone at the small table. Shane set his guitar in the stand and made a beeline for the bar, not sparing a single glance for her as he laughed with the bartender and ordered a beer.

Her chest deflated with her sigh. A man like that would never be interested in someone like her. Even with the extra coat of makeup, her hair and her clothes screamed, "mom." An attractive artist with those long, dexterous fingers, he probably had a different woman in his bed every night, and not one of them had stretchmarks across her hips.

She dug in her purse for her phone to check the time. Heading back to her room now would mean she'd be ready for an early start in the morning. With her gaze cast downward, she caught a glimpse of a pair of black leather boots stopping near her table. Her phone slipped back into her purse as she lifted her head and found Shane standing in front of her. His leather jacket hung open over a dark-gray V-neck T-shirt, and his torn jeans hung low on his hips in typical rock star fashion.

That same crooked, kissable grin tugged on his lips, making heat bloom below her navel. "Hello." He slipped around the side of the table and settled into the empty chair. "I hope I'm not being too forward, but the bartender said you were drinking rosé." A delectable accent lilted his speech as he set the glass of wine in front of her. "I'm Shane."

"You're British." She clamped her mouth shut as heat flushed her cheeks. *Way to go, Captain Obvious. Why don't you tell him he's male too?*

"Guilty." He chuckled. "I'm also a musician, in case you hadn't noticed."

She gazed into his eyes, trying to remember how to form a coherent sentence. A thread of yellow encircled his pupils, shattering in a starburst pattern to blend with the deep green of his irises. The fine lines on the outer edge of his eyes crinkled, deepening as his smile widened.

Swallowing the dryness from her mouth, she pulled herself together. "I'm Bekah."

"Bekah. That's a pretty name." In typical English fashion, he added an imaginary *R* sound to the end of her name, and in typical American girl fashion, her heart fluttered at the sound of his accent. "Is it short for Rebekah?"

"No, it's just Bekah."

"Well, it's nice to meet you, Bekah." If he didn't stop saying her name like that she might start running a fever.

He reached a hand toward her to shake, and she paused, making sure she had her empathic ability in check before accepting the gesture. His magical signature registered on her skin, but nothing more. She'd rather not know his true emotions at the moment.

"Hmm. Are you...?" He held onto her hand a beat longer than necessary.

Her stomach fluttered as she slipped from his grasp. "Second-born. Yes." First-born wolves had a strong signature, but those that couldn't shift gave off a more muddled magic and were often mistaken for witches.

He rubbed his beard and let out an unbelieving chuckle. "Beautiful woman, beautiful name, and a werewolf too. It's no wonder you've piqued my interest."

She ran her finger around the rim of the glass. "Oh, I've piqued your interest, have I?" It had been ages since she'd been the object of anyone's flirtation, but this sure did seem like flirting. A buzzing sensation spread beneath her skin, curving her lips into a smile she couldn't have fought if her life depended on it.

He leaned toward her, resting a forearm on the table. "Very much." He had a warm, woodsy scent mixed with leather and a hint of the sea, and she found herself drifting toward him, drawn in by his presence.

"Yo, Shane. Two minutes," the lead singer called from the stage.

"Bloody hell." He closed his eyes for a long blink and let out an exasperated sigh.

Bekah stifled her giggle, clearing her throat to cover it.

He arched a brow. "Something funny?"

"That's such a British thing to say. 'Bloody hell.' I can't imagine hell being anything but bloody."

"You're making fun of me?" He straightened and took a long drink from his beer, watching her with an amused expression over the bottle as he held it to his lips.

"Not making fun. It's cute."

"Cute?"

"Oh, come on. With your looks alone, you're a ten. Then you open your mouth, and that deep voice with the sexy accent comes out, and women's clothes probably fall off on their own."

He narrowed his eyes, his gaze smoldering as he swept it up and down the length of her. "Yours are still on."

They wouldn't be for long if he kept looking at her like that, and maybe that wasn't such a bad thing. In the ten minutes she'd known the man, he was doing a damn good job of finding the woman in her she'd lost. A sexy musician, one night of passion, and then she'd go home and be a mom again. A little fun wouldn't hurt her.

With her elbow on the table, she rested her chin on her hand. "I guess you'll have to try a little harder if you want them off."

Passion sparked in his eyes so primal it pulled the breath from her lungs. She'd never been so drawn to a man in her entire life, and the temptation to touch him, to use her ability to see if he felt the same, had her fisting her hands in her lap. She wouldn't intrude in his emotions when hers were running so high. She might not be able to separate his from her own.

He slid his arm across the back of her chair and leaned in, his breath warming her ear. "If that's a challenge, love, consider it accepted."

Oh, lord, what have I done? Her body hummed in

anticipation as she turned her face toward his. "Good luck."

His gaze drifted to her lips. "Won't need it."

"Let's go, Shane. Last set," the drummer called.

He rose and whisked his beer from the table. "You'll stay to the end." The last word didn't lift in a question. "I'm not done talking to you."

"I planned to. I'm not done with you either." She held her breath as his gaze bore into her…hot, steady, strong. His raw sex appeal had her trembling on the inside, but she straightened her spine, congratulating herself for projecting way more confidence than she felt.

"This is our last set. Any requests?"

She glanced at the instruments on the stage. A dozen different jazz tunes flitted through her mind, but their repertoire seemed to be rock and pop, so she dismissed them. "I haven't heard you play the sax yet. Can you do 'Careless Whisper?'"

He arched a brow with an *are you serious?* expression.

"That sax solo has got to be the sexiest piece of music ever written, but if you can't, that's okay."

His heated gaze danced between her eyes and her lips. "Anything for you, love. Consider it done."

CHAPTER THREE

SHANE PICKED UP HIS GUITAR AND STRUMMED the rhythm of the first song of their set. If Bekah wanted "Careless Whisper," he'd play it for her, but he'd save it for the end to make sure she didn't get any ideas about leaving early.

The moment he'd looked into her bright, hazel eyes, he'd been mesmerized. Something deep in his soul began to stir, filling him with a longing he'd never felt before. She'd commanded his wolf's attention, and to satiate his beast, he'd have to get to know her.

As the set went on, Bekah sipped the wine he'd bought her, the intensity of her gaze boring deeper into his soul with each song. She was the only person in the room, and every note he played belonged to her.

He signaled to Cammie to start the beat for Bekah's requested song, and Bekah straightened, a smile lifting her pink lips, lighting her entire face. Dark hair fell across her shoulders as she leaned forward on the table, and as he played the solo, her words rang in his ears: *the sexiest piece of music ever written.* In her modest pink blouse and knee-length skirt, Bekah's sex appeal topped it all. She looked polished and professional. Like a woman who had her shit together and wouldn't drop a man on his ass when he couldn't keep up with her partying.

Bekah's outfit left plenty to the imagination, and man, could he imagine.

His eyes usually closed on instinct as he melded with the music, his body becoming part of the song, but he fought to keep them open as he played, his gaze locked on the gorgeous muse sitting before him. Her eyes wandered from his face to his hands, and she bit her bottom lip as she focused on his fingers splaying across the keys.

As the song came to an end, Ricardo thanked the crowd and concluded the show. Bekah hugged Cammie's cousin and strolled toward the stage, clasping her hands behind her back as she eyed him.

"You're very good. You should do more songs that require the saxophone."

So she liked the sax better than the guitar or keyboard. That said a lot about her taste in music, particularly that it was in line with his own. "I've tried to get them to include a few jazz numbers, but they aren't having it."

"I love jazz."

"Do you?" This woman kept getting better. He tugged the strap from around his neck and put the sax in its case.

She shrugged. "I'm from New Orleans. It's ingrained in my soul."

"That must be an exciting place to live. I've always wanted to go there." He lifted the keyboard from the stand and shoved it in the case, breaking apart his setup as fast as he could.

Bekah crossed her arms and drummed her lavender nails against her bicep. "You play sax, you like jazz, and you've never been to New Orleans? You're missing out."

He paused and regarded her, taking in her beauty. She'd brushed her dark-brown hair behind her shoulders, revealing the elegant sweep of her neck, and a magnetic energy buzzed around her, drawing him to her and making him want nothing more than to take her in his arms and plant his lips on hers. "It seems I'm missing out on more than music in the Big Easy. Maybe I should visit some time."

The muscles in her throat worked as she swallowed, and a hint of uncertainty sparked in her eyes, her confidence slipping briefly before she composed herself. "Maybe you should."

"Maybe I will." He stared into her eyes, enchanted by the little gold and brown flecks shimmering in her irises. He could get lost in eyes like those.

A warm palm slapped his shoulder, breaking the trance. "Load up your gear, man. Let's jet."

Shane jumped from the stage and closed the distance between him and Bekah. When she didn't move away, he couldn't help himself; he had to touch her. Gliding his fingertips down her shoulder, he lightly grasped her elbow and leaned toward her. She smelled like heaven, the light floral fragrance of her shampoo mixing with her pheromones to create an intoxicatingly feminine scent that he wanted to wrap himself up in. "I need to put my things in the van so my mates can leave, but if you have a few minutes, I'd love to buy you another drink."

"Oh." She pressed her lips together, glancing toward the exit, her senses seeming to get the better of her. "I have to drive home in the morning. I don't need to drink anymore."

"Coffee then?" He couldn't let her get away. He needed to get to know her, to see if the message his wolf seemed to be sending was what he thought—he hoped—it was.

"I…" She swept her gaze down the length of him, her nostrils flaring as a mask of determination set in her features. "I suppose I have time for coffee. Decaf."

"Brilliant." He flagged down a waitress and ordered two cups. "I'll be right back. Don't go anywhere."

"I'll be here." Bekah slid into a seat, and he set his sax case on the floor by the empty chair.

Shane hauled his gear to the van and shoved it inside before turning back to the hotel.

Ricardo grabbed his arm. "We're leaving. You with us?"

"I'm not missing this opportunity."

"You're supposed to be considering our deal." Cammie put her hands on her hips. "The full moon is tomorrow. We have to do it then."

He inhaled deeply, furrowing his brow like he was considering their offer. "It's going to be a no for me." Not that saying *yes* had ever crossed his mind. "That woman in there…" He glanced at the door. "She could be the one, and she doesn't look like the touring type. I wish you all the success you deserve, but that life isn't for me."

Cammie rolled her eyes. "Love at first sight doesn't exist."

"It does for werewolves, and I'm not wasting this chance."

"Yeah?" Ricardo crossed his arms. "Well, we started the spell with you in it. We still need—"

"It's fine." Cammie gripped Ricardo's arm. "We'll figure it out without him."

Shane strode across the sidewalk and reached for the doorknob. "Sorry, guys. I hate to let you down, but I think I just found my fate-bound."

"What am I doing?" Bekah clutched her coffee mug and stared at the exit Shane had disappeared through. Emma was at home waiting for her. She should've been in bed resting so she could make the drive home first thing in the morning and get back to her life. Back to being a mom.

A light breeze swept in through the door as Shane opened it, and his green eyes glinted with his smile. Her heart thrummed, her stomach fluttering like a teenager who'd caught the eye of the cutest boy in school. His jeans clung to his muscular thighs as he strode toward her, and he slipped off his jacket to reveal a pair of equally muscular arms.

Emma did have school tomorrow, so she wouldn't be able to see her until the afternoon anyway. Having coffee with the man wouldn't hurt anything.

"Thanks for waiting." Shane slipped into the seat next to her, angling his body so his knee brushed hers.

That innocent touch flipped a switch inside her, sending white-hot electricity buzzing in her core. *Holy crap.* She'd be an idiot to fight an attraction this strong. No way in hell was she going home tomorrow without seeing how things played out tonight with Shane. It had been way too long since anyone had touched her—looked at her—the way he was doing right then.

Play it cool, Bek. Maybe he just wants to talk. "You forgot to take your saxophone."

He reached down and ran his hand along the worn, leather case. "This one stays with me. My mum gave it to me when I was seventeen." A look of surprise flashed in his eyes like he hadn't meant to divulge so much.

"That's sweet." She rested a forearm on the table,

tracing the wood pattern with her finger. "Do your parents still live in the UK?"

"London." He placed his arm on the table next to hers, so close she could feel the heat radiating from his skin. "My dad does. My mum died when I was eighteen."

"I'm sorry."

"It was a long time ago." His eyes smoldered as he leaned toward her, his gaze wandering around her face, lingering on her lips as if he were memorizing her features. No one—not even Tommy—had ever looked at her this way. Shane's expression wavered somewhere between wanting to worship her and needing to consume her, and being the object of this delectable werewolf's attention lit a fire inside her that might burn her to ash.

A man like Shane could easily have any woman he wanted, and here he was, sitting in a hotel bar with *her*, caressing her with his eyes and making her feel things she'd wondered if she'd ever feel again.

Words, Bekah. Talk to the man. She cleared her throat. "I guess you came here for your music? Following your dreams?"

He lowered his gaze before looking into her eyes. "I was following something. What about you? What brings you to the sunny state of Florida?"

"Restauranteur conference. I own the Blue Moon Café in the French Quarter, and I was hoping to pick up some tips. Learn some new insights into the business."

"Tell me more." He leaned in, listening intently as she told him about her waitressing jobs and how she eventually moved up to a management position. She'd always dreamed of owning her own place, so she moved in with her brother and went to college to get her degree in restaurant management. She talked about how she'd opened the place and her trusted manager that was watching over the business while she was here, learning more about the trade.

She told him everything. Well, everything except that she had a daughter. This was a one-night-only performance, and she planned to milk it for all it was worth. She'd never see the man again after tonight. No need to complicate things, so she ignored the pinch of guilt in her chest and laid out the rest of her life for him.

He seemed to hang on her every word, listening to her like he was actually interested as she droned on about her café. She couldn't remember a time she'd ever felt so…heard.

The lights behind the bar dimmed before the stage lights blinked out, and she sucked in a sharp breath. "I've talked the bar into closing time. You must think I'm so self-centered, but really I'm not used to someone listening to me."

He took her hand on the table. "I think you're a fascinating, inspirational woman, who is drilling her way into my heart as we speak."

His words held such sincerity, she nearly dropped her shields and let his emotions in, just to see if it could be true.

But it didn't matter if he was telling the truth. She wasn't looking for a relationship. She simply wanted to feel like a woman again, and he was exactly the kind of man who could get her there.

The lights above them dimmed, and moonlight spilling in through the windows cast the room in a silvery glow.

"I guess that's our cue to leave," she said.

"I suppose it is." But he didn't make a move to get up. Instead, he held her gaze with that smoldering intensity and traced his thumb across her hand.

It appeared he didn't want the night to end any more than she did. *Why not?* "Walk me to my room?"

His gaze nearly set her on fire. "My pleasure."

CHAPTER FOUR

As the elevator door slid open and the maid who had joined them on the ride hung a sharp left down the hallway, Bekah took Shane's hand and turned right toward her room. They'd both been silent on the ride up, the maid's presence stopping her from wrapping herself up in his strong embrace like she wanted to.

He'd put his jacket back on, covering those delectable biceps, but she remembered what they looked like, stretching and flexing beneath his T-shirt as he moved. Her pulse raced as they neared her door. She couldn't wait to touch him, to experience the hard sinew beneath his soft skin. To feel his hands on her body, his tongue on her...

A shiver ran up her spine as she pressed the keycard against the lock. "It's just one night."

He brushed her hair behind her shoulder, running the backs of his fingers along her neck. "Did you say something, love?"

She hadn't meant to say that out loud. "Nothing. Damn keycard's giving me trouble." She shoved the door open and turned to face him, swallowing the dryness from her mouth. "Do you want to come in?"

He inhaled deeply, looking her hard in the eyes, as if trying to decipher her question. It wasn't difficult. Either he wanted her like she wanted him, or he didn't.

Stepping into the room, she tossed her purse on the dresser. "I wouldn't have asked you in if I didn't want you to come." She slipped off her shoes and threw them under a chair. "Your move."

He crossed the threshold in two strides and shut the door behind him. "You're smart, strong, insanely gorgeous, and you know exactly what you want. You're a woman after my own heart, Bekah."

Her stomach fluttered. That was the second time he'd mentioned his heart, and they hadn't even kissed yet. *It's just one night.* He probably said these things to all the women he slept with, and that was fine. They were both consenting adults. She didn't mind being another notch in his bedpost.

But the way he looked at her...like she was the only woman in the world... That fire in his gaze came from somewhere deep inside him, and tiny sparks electrified her heart at the idea that his wolf might want her as much as the man did.

When she didn't respond, he hesitated, flicking his gaze from her to the bed to a chair, and then back to her before clearing his throat.

"You should kiss me now."

He nodded. "Right." Closing the distance between them, he took her face in his hand, gliding his fingers into her hair along her temple and running his thumb over her skin. The intensity in his gaze held her, coaxing open her soul and penetrating to the depths of her being.

She felt naked, exposed, as if he'd reached inside and plucked every thought from her mind and wrapped himself in every emotion she'd ever felt.

As he leaned in and brushed his lips to hers, liquid heat rolled through her veins, converging in her chest as her heart went up in flames. His lips were soft, the coarse hair around his mouth tickling her skin as he cupped the back of her head and slid his other hand to her hip.

Running her hands up his chest, she gripped his shoulders, her head spinning as she parted her lips and brushed her tongue against his.

A possessive growl rumbled in his chest, and he pulled her body to his, enveloping her in his strong embrace and kissing her like there was no tomorrow.

With another growl, he broke the kiss, inhaling deeply as he pulled back to look at her. His eyes narrowed, studying her with an expression of disbelief mixed with pure lust. "Tell me you feel that too."

"I'm feeling a lot of things." Number one being that she needed to get this man naked before she exploded.

She tugged his jacket from his shoulders, and he shrugged out of it, letting it fall to the floor. Then he gripped the fabric at the back of his neck and pulled his shirt over his head, dropping it by the jacket.

Bekah's lips parted on an involuntary gasp as her gaze swept across his magnificent chest. Perfectly-sculpted muscles rippled down his stomach, and his low-hung jeans provided a glimpse of the tantalizing V disappearing into the denim.

He chuckled. "Like what you see, love?"

"Very much." Starting at his stomach, she traced her fingers up his body to cup the back of his neck. The softness of his skin and the tingling magic seeping into her hands sent her pulse racing. The way he held her to his chest, dipping his tongue into her mouth, his hands roaming her body, gripping her like he couldn't hold her close enough... She'd never felt so wanted in her entire life.

And there was entirely too much fabric between them.

Never breaking contact with his body, she pressed her hips into his, arching her back and lifting her shirt over her head.

An appreciative grunt sounded from his throat as he lowered his gaze to her chest and cupped her breasts in his hands. His hooded gaze bore into her as he teased her nipples through her bra, and she reached behind her back to snap open the clasp.

The straps slid off her shoulders, and he tossed the garment aside. "Magnificent."

Dipping his head, he flicked out his tongue, bathing her nipple in wet heat. As he sucked it into his mouth, his teeth grazing the sensitive flesh, electricity zinged to her middle, tightening her stomach, her body aching with desire.

He moved to her other breast, taking the nipple between his lips and circling his tongue over the hardened tip. The sensation was maddening, and she tangled her fingers in his dark hair as a moan emanated from her throat.

As he glided his lips up her chest to nip at her neck, he reached behind her, tugging at her zipper and working her skirt over her hips. The garment fell to the floor, and he stepped back, taking in the length of her with his eyes.

She cringed inwardly, fighting the urge to cover her stomach, expecting his gaze to linger on the pooch of baby weight she'd never lost or for the desire in his eyes to fizzle out as he took in the stretch marks arcing over her hips.

But the longing intensified as he moved toward her, wrapping her in a consuming embrace and kissing her like she *belonged* to him.

Like his wolf was claiming her.

Her blood fizzed at the thought, her entire body lighting up like a Fourth of July fireworks display.

She fumbled with the button on his jeans, and he stilled her hands, leaning back just far enough to look into her eyes.

"Are you on birth control?"

"Yes."

"Is this what you want?"

Her heart pounded in her throat. His warm, woodsy scent filled her senses, and her need for this man occupied every thought her mind would form. "I want you, Shane."

"Then you'll have me, love." He toed off his boots and pulled down his jeans, kicking them aside before removing the rest of his clothes. As he stood before her, naked and rock hard all over, he spread his arms to his sides. "I'm yours."

"Yes, you are." She snaked her hands behind his neck and took his mouth in a kiss. The feel of his warm body pressed to hers was almost too much to bear, achingly intimate, yet she couldn't seem to get close enough to him.

Sensing her urgency, he grabbed her ass, lifting her from the floor, and she cinched her legs around his waist as they fell to the bed. He showered her face and neck in kisses, rocking his hips and rubbing his cock against her center, but her cotton panties blocked him, dulling the sensation she so desperately needed to feel.

"You are so beautiful, Bekah." The imaginary *R* he added at the end of her name made her shiver, and he trailed his lips across her collar bone, down between her breasts and toward her stomach as he slowly slid to his knees on the floor.

Resting his chin near her navel, he gazed up at her, roaming his hands over her body, caressing every inch of her bare skin. He circled his tongue around her belly button, gliding it down to the edge of her panties, leaving a trail of fire everywhere he touched.

She held her breath as he slipped her underwear off, tossing them aside before running his hands up the insides of her thighs. Clutching her hips, he tugged her toward the edge of the bed and draped her legs over his shoulders.

Her body trembled, anticipation coiling in her core as his warm breath danced across her skin. He slipped out his tongue, bathing her sensitive nub in wet warmth, sending a shock of electricity ricocheting through her body.

She gasped, and a sensual moan rumbled in his throat as he gripped her hips, diving into her center and lapping at her as if his sole purpose in life were to pleasure her. He knew exactly what to do, where to touch, the perfect pressure and rhythm to drive her wild.

She clutched the sheets, arching her back as her climax built, crying out as her orgasm crested like a wave, crashing into her, drowning her in passion.

As he slowed his pace, he lightened the pressure of his tongue, bringing her down slowly before rising and pressing a kiss to her stomach, between her breasts, and to her mouth. "The sounds you make when I pleasure you are more beautiful than any music I've ever heard."

Heat crept up her neck, and she pulled him down for another kiss, reaching her hand between them to grip his dick. "I need you inside me, Shane."

He rose onto his hands, pinning her with a heated gaze that said he wanted to consume her...and she couldn't wait to be devoured.

She scooted from the edge of the bed to lie in the center, and he moved with her, covering her with his body, his gaze never straying from hers. As she stroked his cock, his eyelids fluttered, and with a long exhale, he settled his hips between her legs.

He pressed against her, his tip barely penetrating her folds as he held his weight on his arms. She needed him. God, she ached to feel him inside her, filling her. He pushed in a little farther, so torturously, wonderfully slow she wanted to scream. He wasn't hesitating...rather savoring each delicious inch he took.

The intensity in his gaze grew heavier the deeper he slid inside her, making this moment feel like something...more. "This is it, love."

As his hips met hers and he filled her completely, a sense of wholeness fell over her. He lowered his body to hers, sliding his hands beneath her shoulders to hold her, clutching her to his chest as he moved.

He slid in and out, slowly at first, but increasing in both speed and intensity as the passion overtook them. She gripped his back, clinging to him, wrapping her legs around his waist as another climax coiled inside her, and he growled, burying his face in her neck as he pumped his hips furiously.

Lightning surged in her core, releasing a storm of emotion as her orgasm ripped through her body, her muscles shuddering beneath his weight, and her shields slipped. Shane's emotions seeped into her, flooding her heart with passion, ecstasy, and... *No, it couldn't be.*

There, in the mix of desire and lust, she felt his wolf, and the beast had one word on its mind: *Mine.*

Shane groaned, pressing into her as his own climax consumed him, before relaxing on top of her, his fingers slowly releasing their grip on her shoulders. He nuzzled into her, a feeling of utter happiness emanating from his skin, filling her with a sense of unfounded joy.

This wasn't happening. His wolf was not claiming her.

She slid her shields back into place, blocking Shane's emotions from her consciousness. She knew better than to try to read someone she was close to like this. When her own emotions ran high, her senses were easily clouded. She hadn't actually felt his wolf claiming her. That was a product of her imagination.

In the couple of hours she'd known Shane, he'd made her feel more important, more wanted, more needed than she'd felt in her entire life. She'd be thrilled if a man like him wanted to claim her. Who wouldn't be?

Her own fanciful desires were muddling her perception, so she would forget her shields had ever slipped.

He was enjoying the night with her like she was enjoying it with him, and tonight was all they would ever have.

She'd made the mistake of confusing her own emotions with her boyfriend's in the past. She wouldn't let it happen again.

Shane's muscles felt like jelly as he rolled onto his back and pulled Bekah to his side. She laid her head on his pec, draping her leg over his hips and resting her hand on his opposite shoulder, her body conforming to his like the final piece of a puzzle clicking into place.

She was made for him. Made to fit in his arms, to be in his life. He kissed the top of her head and breathed in the sweet, clean fragrance of her shampoo, the warm undercurrent that was uniquely Bekah awakening his wolf, bringing the beast to the surface.

Mine.

There was no sense in fighting this. The timing couldn't have been more perfect, but such was the nature of fate. The stars had aligned and were shining down on him, sending the message loud and clear.

He'd found his fate-bound.

He tightened his arms around her, memorizing the way her body felt wrapped up in his embrace. She belonged with him, and based on the way they'd made love, she felt it too.

She lifted her head to look at him, a sleepy smile tugging at her lips as she pressed a kiss to the corner of his mouth. Propping her head on her hand, she glided her fingers across his chest. "You never told me what brought you to Florida. Following the music?"

He placed his hand on top of hers, holding it to his chest. "I was following a girl."

Surprise flashed in her eyes. "All the way from the UK? She must have been pretty special."

He chuckled. "She thought she was."

"What happened?"

What the hell? His wolf had already claimed her, and he planned to eventually take her as his mate. He might as well lay it all out for her. "About five years ago, I fell in love with a human." He held her gaze, gauging her reaction to decide if he should hold back.

When she didn't flinch, he continued, "Let me rephrase that. I *thought* I was in love with a human, but I was young and dumb, and my wolf wasn't the slightest bit interested in her, but..."

"Been there." She laughed. "Not with a human, but the young and dumb part. So she moved here, and you followed her?"

"Worse than that. I played in her band."

She lifted her eyebrows, urging him to continue.

"She got an American recording contract, so she moved to LA. I came with her and played lead guitar. We toured all over the US, sleeping in a different hotel room every night, never really calling anywhere home."

"That sounds exciting."

"It gets old fast, believe me. The parties, the drinking, the drugs. She was living the rock star life-style, but all I wanted to do was stay in one place more than a few days at a time. She tired of me quickly when I stopped partying with her."

"Couldn't keep up?" She flashed a teasing smile.

"I'm a werewolf. I could drink her under the table, and it drove her mad when I'd be up at dawn the next day while she nursed her hangover until midafternoon. Anyway, after a while, she fell *in* love with those white, powdery lines, and fell *out* of love with me. We played a show in Orlando, and she dumped me straight after. Kicked me out of the band and left me there with nothing but my saxophone for company."

"Ouch. That sucks."

He shrugged. "It did for a while, but I got over it. I met Ricardo and Cammie and joined their band. We do local shows, all in-state. It's a slower pace, but it suits me."

"Do you ever think about going home to London? Back to your pack and your family?"

He started to tell her he'd never been in a pack, that his parents had always been rogues, but he thought better of it. Bekah had mentioned that her brother was second in command of the New Orleans pack when she'd told him her life story in the bar, and he had no idea how she felt about rogues. Better to let her get to know him before she had the chance to form judgments.

"If my mum were alive, I might consider it."

"What happened to her? I mean...if you don't mind telling me." Her eyes held so much compassion he couldn't fathom holding anything else back.

"She was in the wrong place at the wrong time. Got caught in a convenience shop robbery and was shot in the heart." His throat thickened, and he pushed the memory aside. Now was not the time for reminiscing about his past. Not when he held his future in his arms.

"I'm so sorry, Shane." She bit her bottom lip.

"It's okay, love. Like I said, it was a long time ago. Anyway, my father disowned me when I left for America, so there's no point in going back." Maybe he shouldn't have told her that part, but it was out there now, and she didn't pull away.

"Why would he do that?"

He searched her eyes for judgment, but all he found was concern. Usually, people only wanted to hear about his time on tour. When the conversation shifted to his personal life, most women got bored, their eyes glazing if they couldn't steer the subject back to Shane the rocker.

Bekah was actually interested in the man. *Of*

course she is, wanker. She's your fate-bound. "My mum was a music teacher. She taught me everything I know; I can play any instrument I get my hands on. Music is ingrained in my soul, but my father wanted me to pick a more 'useful' profession."

"It was okay with him for your mom to teach music, but not for you to perform?"

"He's a…" The word rogue almost slipped out, but he bit it back. "He's independent. Thinks music is for women and… I won't use his words, but not for masculine men, you know?"

"Gotcha. Well, I think musicians can be very masculine." She kissed him, lingering near his lips until he couldn't help but kiss her again. He dipped his tongue into the wet warmth of her mouth, and a shiver ran down his spine. Oh, yes. This woman belonged with him.

She pulled back, her gaze dancing around his face. "Our alpha can play piano, believe it or not."

"Considering it's New Orleans, I believe it." Which was another reason the stars were shining on him tonight. His fate-bound lived in the birthplace of jazz. He couldn't think of a better place to settle down and live his dream. "In answer to your question, no, I never think about going back to London, but I am planning to see New Orleans soon."

Her expression darkened, her brow furrowing as she chewed her bottom lip. Not the reaction he was expecting, but maybe she didn't understand what he was saying.

He cupped her cheek in his hand. "I have to see you again."

She shook her head and sat up, clutching a pillow in her lap. "Shane, you and I both know what this was, so you don't have to make promises you don't intend to keep. I'm not delusional. I know I'm never going to see you again."

He sat up too. "You are delusional if you think a one-night stand is all I want from you. Bekah, this is the start of something, not the end."

She studied him, narrowing her eyes as if trying to decide if she should believe him.

"Earlier, when I said 'this is it,' I meant this is *it*. The beginning of a relationship. I have to see you again, and if that means going to New Orleans, then that's what I'll do."

She smiled and loosened her grip on the pillow. "I'd like that."

"Yeah?" His heart pounded in his chest.

"Yeah."

"Good." His phone rang from somewhere in the heap of clothes on the floor, but he ignored it.

Confliction clouded her eyes as she scooted to the edge of the bed. "If you're sure about this...about coming to New Orleans to see me..."

"I've never been more sure of anything in my life."

The corners of her mouth twitched like she wanted to smile again. "There's something you need to know about me. I..." She blew out a hard breath. "I have a kid."

His heart took a nosedive into his stomach. *Oh, hell.* Had his wolf claimed someone who was spoken for? "Do you have a boyfriend?"

"No." She shook her head adamantly. "It's a long story, but I got pregnant when I was nineteen. Emma's father is a witch, but he left as soon as he found out, and I haven't seen him since. I'm not... I just wanted you to know, in case you want to change your mind."

He tucked a strand of hair behind her ear. "Why would I want to change my mind?"

She drew her shoulders up. "She's my first-born. She's only eight, so I don't know if she'll be a shifter yet or not. Before you start making plans to see where this goes with you and me, you need to know what you're getting into. What it could mean for...the future. Your lineage."

He sucked in a breath as the realization dawned on him. She was trying to tell him his first-born wouldn't be her first-born, so he may not have a shifting child of his own. "I don't give a damn about my lineage. Do you want to know what I want out of life?"

She nodded.

"I don't think I've ever told anyone this before, but…" He chuckled. "I want to settle down someday and have my own music school like my mum. I want to teach kids the love of music, and I want to have a few kids of my own. Whether or not they can shift isn't important to me." He simply wanted to love them. To be everything his father never was for him. To be dependable.

"Are you sure?"

"I—" The phone rang again, and he glanced toward his pants.

"You can answer. It could be your pack."

He hesitated, glancing between the ringtone and Bekah, but she motioned with her hand for him to take the call. Rolling out of bed, he dug in his pocket and checked the screen. Ricardo. "Bloody hell." He pressed the device to his ear. "It's three a.m."

"Cammie's passed out."

He crept into the bathroom and lowered his voice. "That happens when she drinks too much."

"No, man." Ricardo's voice sounded frantic. "It's the spell. She was working on it, and...we need you. She was trying to continue it without you, but she can't remove you from it without you here." A muffled *bang* sounded in the distance. "Something happened to her, and she blacked out. Can you get over here? I think I can revive her if we're all present. The guys are on their way."

Damn it, these witches had the worst timing. "All right, mate. I'll come, you'll remove me from the whole ordeal, and then I'm done. Got it?"

"Yeah, yeah. Just get here as fast as you can." Ricardo ended the call, and Shane fought the urge to hurl his phone across the room. *Stupid witches.*

He shuffled into the bedroom and found Bekah picking up his clothes, turning them right side out. "I have to go."

She shrugged and smiled. "I figured as much. When the pack calls, we answer, right?"

"Right." No need to explain the predicament he was in. He'd be done with the witches soon enough. "What time are you leaving tomorrow?"

She handed him his pants and picked up his shirt, righting it as she spoke. "I was planning to leave first thing in the morning, but I could stick around a little longer if…"

"Good. Get some rest, and I'll be back at ten a.m. We'll have a late breakfast and figure out a plan for when I can see you again." He took his shirt from her hands and slipped it over her head. "And you can wear this while I'm gone, so you don't forget about me."

She laughed and put her arms through the sleeves. "I don't think I could ever forget about you." She lifted the fabric to her nose and inhaled deeply, closing her eyes as if reveling in the scent.

His stomach tightened, his dick hardening at the thought of her reveling in him. He put his jacket on and stepped into his boots before pulling her into a tight embrace. "I'll be back before you know it, love."

"Here." She slipped a ring of dark-gray beads around his wrist. A lighter gray, iridescent marble pattern ran through the polished stones, glinting in the lamplight. "So you don't forget about *me* while you're gone."

He examined the bracelet, holding onto Bekah with his free hand. His wolf didn't want to let her go. Neither did the man. "This is pretty."

"It's a clarity bracelet that my sister-in-law made

for me. It's supposed to help you focus on the most important things in your life."

His chest tightened. He didn't need a bracelet to tell him what he wanted out of life, and he was finally on his way to having it all. He pressed a kiss to her lips and reluctantly let her go. "I'll see you soon, Bekah."

CHAPTER FIVE

BEKAH SAT ON THE EDGE OF THE BED, clutching her keys in her hands and watching the little red numbers on the clock face flip from ten forty-five to forty-six, forty-seven. Her nostrils flared as she let out a slow breath, the reality of the situation pressing on her shoulders, shame making heat creep up her neck and bloom across her cheeks.

She should have seen this coming. Hot guys like Shane weren't looking to settle down, especially not with a single mom who lived in another state. As if he'd follow her to New Orleans.

In her defense, he did say he followed a girl here all the way from the UK. What were a few hundred miles when he'd crossed an entire ocean before? Especially after what she'd thought she felt from him…

She picked up his shirt and pressed it to her nose, inhaling his woodsy, masculine scent. It still made her stomach flutter, even though he'd stood her up. She groaned and shoved the shirt into her suitcase.

Everything had been fine until he started filling her head with false promises, making her believe what she felt in him had been real. She was prepared for a one-night stand. She'd *wanted* it to be a one-night stand. All she'd needed was for him to help her feel like a woman again, and he'd done a bang-up job of that.

She shivered at the memory of his hands on her body, and the way he worked his tongue. But then, in the heat of passion, the emotions she'd felt in him were beyond her wildest expectations. Strong, primal, possessive.

She'd felt something similar when she read her brother after he met his fate-bound, and then when she felt it coming from Shane...

Well, she *thought* she'd felt the emotions from Shane. Obviously, her own desires had overpowered his actual emotions, and that was no surprise. She hadn't had a clue when Tommy freaked out about Emma. When she'd told him she was pregnant, he'd acted happy, which had made her happy in return.

And even when she'd attempted to read the

bastard, her own emotions had clouded her ability, making it impossible to tell what he was really feeling. That Tommy had planned to disappear as soon as she fell asleep.

She couldn't trust her ability when her own emotions were involved. She *knew* that, but it didn't ease the stabbing pain in her heart. Zipping her suitcase, she rose to her feet and wheeled it out the door. Check-out ended at eleven, and she was out of time.

She hit the button for the elevator and ground her teeth. Shane left without asking for her number. That should have been a red flag, but she'd been so high on the stupid fated mates idea she hadn't even considered that she had no way to contact him.

The doors slid open, and she held her breath, hoping maybe…

The space stood empty. She blew out a breath and stepped into the elevator, determined to put Shane and all his beautiful, empty promises out of her mind.

Bekah picked up Emma from her grandma's house that afternoon, and after three days, life in New Orleans returned to normal. She ran her café, slowly implementing the new techniques she'd learned at the conference, and though it took her a few days, she was able to forgive the befuddled ending to her night with Shane and relish the memory of feeling alive again for the first time in years.

He'd merely proven himself the asshole she'd expected him to be. No reason to hold a grudge against a man she'd never see again. No harm was done, and it had been plenty of fun at the time.

"Bekah." Dani, the head server, knocked on the office door, pulling her from her thoughts. "Oooh, what are you grinning about? I wanna see." She pranced around the desk, scowling as she glimpsed the spreadsheet on the computer screen. "That's nothing to smile at."

Bekah laughed. "Sorry to disappoint. What's up?"

"Oh." Dani adjusted her ponytail and stepped around the desk. "There's a guy out on the patio; he's been here about an hour but hasn't ordered anything. He looks like he might be homeless, and he seems pretty confused too. Do you want me to send him away or call the cops?"

Bekah cringed. Most of the homeless knew the rules: if they didn't order something, they didn't get to occupy the tables. But if he was new in town, he might need to be clued in to the way things worked.

"Don't call the cops yet. I'll come out and talk to him."

"You got it, boss." Dani gave her a mock salute. "He could be a hottie if he cleaned himself up and got off whatever he's taking that makes him so spaced out."

She sighed, rising to her feet, and followed her employee through the dining room and out onto the patio. Dani thought any man with eyes and a heartbeat could be a hottie, so Bekah wasn't expecting much.

The man sat at a table near the edge of the patio, looking out across the street. His black leather jacket and mop of dark hair stopped Bekah in her tracks. Her heart dipped into her stomach before lodging into her throat as Dani tapped him on his shoulder.

"This is Bekah, the café owner. She'd like to speak to you." Dani gestured toward her, and the man turned around as Dani scurried off to clean up the coffee a customer spilled on the floor.

His sea-green eyes pierced her soul like the first time they'd met, and for a moment, the fact that he'd stood her up didn't matter, and her heart filled with hope. Shane had come to New Orleans.

"Shane?" Her body lightened, and she rose onto

her toes as she drifted toward him. "What are you doing here?"

His brow pinched, a strange look clouding his eyes as he blinked at her and glanced at his saxophone case. "You're Bekah?"

The bubble of hope in her chest sprang a leak, and she put her hands on her hips. "Who else would I be?"

"Bekah," he muttered and studied the menu on the table. "Blue Moon Café."

"What's going on?" A sense of unease washed over her, souring her stomach.

He lifted his gaze to hers and tilted his head. "I'm sorry, love. Do I know you?"

Her jaw dropped open, her eyes going wide as he twisted a knife in her heart. "Are you kidding me? Is this some kind of joke?" A couple at a table across the patio looked at her, and she took a deep breath to compose herself, lowering her voice to a whisper. "What are you doing, Shane?"

He shook his head, acting like he seriously didn't remember her, a cocky smile lighting on his lips. "Bekah. Blue Moon Café."

Resting a hand on the table, she leaned in closer to him, a spark of anger igniting in her core. He smelled like he hadn't showered since she'd seen him three days ago, but that warm, woodsy undercurrent peeked through, his pheromones still calling to her, making her body react against her will.

She bent to his eye level. "Yes, I'm Bekah from the Blue Moon Café. The woman you slept with and made beautiful promises of beginnings and things to come." She fisted her hands to stop herself from grabbing a handful of his jacket and shoving him off the patio. "I was fine with a one-night stand. You didn't have to say all those things, you sick bastard."

His lips parted on a quick inhale, but she wasn't about to let him get another word in.

"You've been sitting here for an hour. Either order something or stop taking up space in my café." She straightened and crossed her arms over her chest. "What's it going to be?"

He glanced about the café before clearing his throat. "I seem to have misplaced my wallet." His smile returned, fueling the fire of her anger.

"Get out, Shane."

"I don't have any money, love. I'm not sure where to go."

She fought her eye-roll. "You have the gall to come to my café, pretend like you don't remember me, and then tell me you have nowhere to go? What? You think I'm going to take you in? Give you money?" Her body shook with anger. "Why don't you take your saxophone and go play 'Careless Whisper' on the street? I'm sure the tourists will help you out with some cash."

He blinked, flinching as if he'd been slapped. "The sexiest piece of music ever written."

Her blood boiled. "Get. Out."

He hesitated, his mouth hanging open.

"Leave, Shane. Don't come back."

He grabbed his sax case and rose to his feet, shaking his head and muttering, "Bekah. Blue Moon Café," still pretending like he had no idea who she was.

What an ass. As he crossed the sidewalk into the street, Bekah turned on her heel and marched into the dining room.

A tiny voice in the back of her mind screamed at her to stop him. Damn it, even after that tenacious display of assholery, she was still attracted to him. *Get a grip.*

She shook her hands, trying to rid herself of the lightning sparking inside her. *He's an asshole, just like you thought he'd be. Deal with it.*

"Aw. You got rid of Hottie Homeless Guy?" Dani stopped in front of her, carrying a tray of empty coffee mugs. "Did you notice he was shirtless beneath that sexy leather jacket? Six pack and everything."

No, she did not notice that. She'd been too focused on all the ridiculous emotions swirling through her own body, tunneling her vision. She hadn't paid attention to anything but his eyes at the time, but now that Dani mentioned it, he seemed to be wearing the same clothes he'd had on when he left her hotel room. There was no telling what a guy like that could've gotten himself into.

It didn't matter. She was done with Shane. "If he comes back, call the cops. I'm not dealing with him again."

Shane knew her.

She was important somehow, but every time a fuzzy memory began to form, it dissolved into mist. *This is bloody frustrating.* He raked a hand through his hair, pulling it at the roots as he crossed the street, moving away from the café.

The Blue Moon Café.

The place was important too, but he couldn't for the life of him remember why. He hung a left and paced up the sidewalk, wracking his brain for a memory of...anything. Hell, the only reason he knew his name was Shane was because of the engraved plate on the saxophone case. Even then, he wasn't sure the name belonged to him until Bekah said it.

Other than his name and the fact that he apparently slept with the beautiful café owner, he couldn't remember a bloody thing. He'd learned from the address on the menu that he was in New Orleans. That seemed important too, but he had no idea how he got there, if he lived there...or if he didn't, where he came from.

Nothing.

But the memories were there. They danced around his consciousness, teasing him with blurry images and feelings of recognition before darting away the moment he tried to grab onto one.

Bekah was there, somewhere in the void of his mind, but she also ran deeper, into his soul. Something about her resonated with him. His wolf recognized her. Though the beast's memories were as clouded as his own, the moment their eyes had met, his wolf had stirred. The animal became restless, and the urge to take her in his arms, to protect her from...something...had overwhelmed him.

He paused on a street corner and held the sax case in both hands. When Bekah mentioned that song...

"Careless Whisper"…it jarred loose a memory. Her teasing smile. A passionate gaze. The words *the sexiest piece of music ever written* had come from somewhere.

He needed to take stock. Figure out what he did know, and then he could work on recalling what he'd lost. He knew how to play the instrument, of that he was sure. And Bekah…

A shudder ran through his body at the thought of her. She was the key to everything; he could feel it in his bones. Remembering her was his top priority.

He closed his eyes and focused on the sliver of memory her mention of the song had provided. He saw her face, her smile. That song meant something to them, and he had to figure out what it was.

Two women stopped in front of a shop window, the brunette taking her phone from her purse and swiping at the screen. Shane zipped his jacket closed —finding a shirt should be his next priority—and strolled toward them, putting on his most charming smile. "Excuse me, I wonder if you could help a bloke out."

The woman's brows shot up, a slight wariness tightening her eyes before she relaxed into a smile. "You're British."

The flush of irritation in his chest told him he

probably got that response a lot. "I seem to have misplaced my phone, and I got a request for a song I'm unfamiliar with. I was hoping you could look it up for me."

She tapped her screen. "Sure, what's it called?"

"The song is 'Careless Whisper.' I'm not sure of the artist."

The woman laughed and glanced at her friend. "Are you yanking my chain? You're British, and you're *unfamiliar* with Wham!?" She made air quotes with her fingers.

He bit back his frustration and forced a smile. "I'm afraid I'm not a big fan of pop music."

The woman shook her head. "George Michael? You must know him."

Clenching his teeth, he let out a slow breath. Perhaps there was a music store nearby. He'd find another way to hear the song. "Thank you for your time. I'm sorry to bother you." He nodded and turned to walk away.

"Wait," the woman called. "Here it is." She held her phone toward him, and a man's voice drifted through the air.

Shane focused on the rhythm, closing his eyes and allowing the music to seep into his soul. Familiarity buzzed around his senses, the tune becoming more recognizable as the singer crooned on. When the saxophone solo played, something in his mind snapped. Another memory wiggled free from its confines, presenting itself to him like a movie.

In his mind, Shane stood on stage playing this same riff. He'd fought to keep his eyes open while he played because Bekah watched him from the audience, a sultry smile and a look of longing in her eyes.

That was it. He'd played the song for *her*. Maybe if he played it for her again…

He opened his eyes and nodded at the woman. "Thank you, so very much."

Shane darted across the street, and a car slammed on its brakes, laying on the horn as he narrowly missed being flattened by the front end. He tapped the hood and waved an apology before stepping onto the sidewalk and heading back to the café. To Bekah.

He stopped outside the entrance, set the case on the ground, and slipped the strap on his saxophone over his head. Attaching the mouthpiece, he positioned the reed, tightening it into place before drumming his fingers across the keys. The instrument felt so natural in his hands, like he'd played it a thousand times, though he couldn't remember any of them.

Any but one. Playing for Bekah.

He ran the tune through his mind, fingering the

keys as he thought about the melody. He remembered how to form every note, yet he couldn't recall where he'd slept last night. A glance through the café window showed Bekah behind the counter, handing a takeaway order to a customer. She didn't want him inside her restaurant, but the sidewalk outside was a public area.

He brought the reed to his lips and blew into the instrument, belting out the song flawlessly. He didn't have to think about the music; it was as natural to him as breathing. As he played, the fog in his mind began to lift, his night with Bekah coming into clear view.

Their flirtatious banter at a bar had turned into a passionate night between the sheets. With his eyes closed, the image of Bekah filled his mind, stirring in his heart and awakening a feeling so strong it was a wonder how it had been buried with his memories.

He burned for her, and being with her had made him feel like his life was complete. His wolf hovered near the surface as he played, and a single word echoed in his head.

Mine.

CHAPTER SIX

As a customer opened the café door, a familiar song drifted inside, making Bekah's breath catch. She finished ringing up a to-go order and padded around the counter to the window.

Her pulse thrummed. Shane stood outside, "Careless Whisper" flowing from his saxophone with the same soulful intensity she remembered from the night they met. *What kind of game is he playing?* Her hands curled into fists, and her emotions battled over swooning for the man all over again and wanting to wring his neck for putting her through this.

She focused on the anger and marched out the door, intent on giving him a piece of her mind. But as she stood in front of him, watching him play, his eyes closed, his body moving as if the music were a part of him, the urge to swoon clawed its way to the top.

She forced the ridiculous emotions down and crossed her arms, waiting for the song to end. "What do you think you're doing?"

Shane opened his eyes. "I played that song for you the night we met."

"Oh, you remember now? Isn't that nice?" She tapped her foot.

"I do, Bekah." He stepped toward her, but she stepped back. His shoulders slumped, and he swallowed hard. "Can we talk somewhere private?"

"I've got nothing to say to you."

"Then listen, please." He reached for her, and her bracelet peeked from his sleeve.

Her throat thickened as she raked her gaze over his disheveled form. She'd been so caught up in her anger at being stood up, she hadn't stopped to consider his side of the story. From the way he looked, something had happened to him between then and now. "Please tell me what's going on. Why did you act like you didn't remember me?"

"Because I didn't." His green eyes held her gaze, pleading with her to understand. "I don't...I *didn't* remember anything. My mind..." He waved his hand around his head. "I've lost my memory, Bekah." As the crowd that had formed around him while he played dispersed, he tried again to move closer to her, and this time she let him.

"What happened? Where have you been?"

"I don't know. I don't…" He let out a frustrated sigh. "I don't know who I am. I can't remember where I'm from nor how I got here. All I know is that I found your café. I found you. Somewhere in the void of my mind, you were there, and I found you. And seeing you again, it didn't register at first, until you mentioned the song. Then an image broke free, and that image was of you, smiling at me, and I knew you were important."

He raked a hand through his hair and shook his head. "Playing the music helped me, but the only thing I can remember is you. Do you know why that is?"

"I don't…no." A hummingbird took flight in her stomach.

"You're my fate-bound, Bekah. My wolf has claimed you, and I think you feel it too. I know you do."

She sucked in a sharp breath, her fingers covering her lips as she searched his eyes. What she was looking for, she wasn't sure. She did feel it too. She'd felt it the moment they'd met, but she'd blamed it on her hormones and the fact that she hadn't been with a man since Emma was born.

Reaching a trembling hand toward him, she gripped his wrist, opening her sixth sense and letting his emotions flow into her. Confusion, despair, and determination swirled through his psyche, but in the middle of it all, steady and strong as iron, she felt his wolf…and his wolf *had* claimed her.

"Wait here." She pushed open the door but paused and looked at him. "Don't leave."

He smiled. "I'm not going anywhere without you, love."

The hummingbird wings beating against her stomach multiplied into a swarm as she rushed through the dining room and into the office. She grabbed her purse from her desk drawer and found her assistant manager in the kitchen. "I have to cut out early today. Can you hold down the fort?"

"No problem. Everything okay?"

"It will be." She turned on her heel and flew through the front door, finally slowing down to breathe when she found Shane leaning against the wall, the sax case at his feet.

"Come with me." She took his hand and led him away from the café.

"Where are we going?" He strode beside her, a

sense of relief loosening the tension in his broad shoulders.

"To my place so we can talk." They walked in silence toward her house as Bekah attempted to corral her thoughts. A brisk breeze blew down the street, mussing her hair, and she rubbed at the goose bumps on her arms.

Shane's gaze flitted around at the scenery, his expression ranging from confusion to the wide-eyed look of awe at his surroundings. As they passed through Jackson Square, he stared at the massive St. Louis Cathedral, with its off-white façade and triple steeples, until a street performer juggling fire batons drew his attention.

She guided him out of the square, deeper into the French Quarter, toward the residential area. A three-piece band struck up a jazzy tune on a street corner, and Shane paused, tilting his head as he watched them play.

"Almost there." Bekah tugged him around the corner, onto a street lined with one and two-story Creole cottages painted in shades ranging from gray to bright purple. Her mind raced as they approached her house, a deep brown, shotgun-style home with dark-blue trim.

She unlocked the front door, ushering him inside. "What's the last thing you remember?"

He set his case down and swept his gaze around her open living room and kitchen area. "I remember you. Not much else."

"Do you remember your bandmates? Your family? Anything?"

He squeezed his eyes shut and pinched the bridge of his nose. "I don't, but I know I should. I can feel the memories. They're in my mind, but I can't access them."

"I don't know what happened to you, but I'm going to help you figure it out. First, though, you need to clean yourself up. I don't think you've showered since we met." She guided him through the kitchen and pointed out the bathroom. "There's an extra toothbrush in the drawer. I'll wash your clothes while you're in the shower."

He looked around at the bathroom before pinning her with his gaze. "Thank you, Bekah, for believing me. I don't know who I can trust right now, except for you." He shrugged out of his jacket and popped the button on his jeans.

His body was as sculpted as she remembered, and heat pooled below her navel as she stepped into the hallway and pulled the door halfway shut. "Just...toss your clothes out here and I'll throw them in the wash. Towels are in the linen closet." She couldn't handle seeing him naked right now. *Focus on what's important.*

He reached his hands through the open space in the doorway, offering her the pile of clothes. "I appreciate your hospitality."

Oh boy. She took the clothes and padded to the laundry room as the bathroom door clicked shut. His pockets were empty, so she shoved his clothes into the machine and set it on the quick-wash cycle before shuffling to the living room.

Think, Bekah. Focus. At the rate werewolves could heal, even a massive blow to the head wouldn't cause complete amnesia. If he'd gotten in a car accident when he left her hotel room, he wouldn't have made it all the way to New Orleans. Unless he hitchhiked. An accident didn't feel right though. Someone did this to him, and she was going to find out who.

She paced a line from the kitchen to the living room, wringing her hands and trying to concentrate on the situation, but she couldn't focus. Sinking onto the couch, she smiled. Shane's wolf had claimed her; she hadn't imagined it.

Giddy laughter bubbled from her chest, and she covered her mouth to muffle it. She'd found her soulmate. He couldn't remember a single thing about his life, but he remembered her. He belonged to her.

A wave of dizziness forced her to squeeze her eyes shut. She hadn't seen this coming. Had she known her attempt at a one-night stand would turn into a lifelong, soul-deep connection, she would have...

Well, what would you have done, Bek? Fate hadn't given her a choice in the matter and she had Emma to consider. Her daughter may not take to Shane, and what then? Surely fate wouldn't bind her heart to someone her daughter wouldn't like. That's if fate even considered other people when bringing two souls together.

The washing machine buzzed, signaling the end of the cycle, and she moved his clothes to the dryer. A few minutes later, Shane emerged from the bathroom, wearing nothing but a dark-blue towel wrapped around his waist.

Her fingers twitched, the memory of his soft skin and hard...everything...awakening a feral desire deep inside her. She wanted to go to him. To take him in her arms and tell him everything would be okay and kiss away the worry etching canyons into his forehead.

She bit the inside of her cheek to keep herself grounded. He was in a dangerous situation. They had no clue who had wiped his memory nor why, and him being here...while everything about him being here felt so right, he may have brought the danger into her pack, into her home.

"Your clothes should be dry in about twenty minutes."

"Thank you." He ran a hand through his damp hair, brushing it away from his face, and his biceps bunched, flexing with the movement.

Her gaze wandered from his muscular arms, down his stomach, toward his... She had to get some clothes on this man before she lost control.

"Just a second." She marched into her bedroom and dug some garments from her dresser. "You can put these on while you wait." She handed him the stack of clothes, and he followed her into the living room.

"Whose are these?" He tugged the shirt over his head and stepped into the sweat pants, pulling them up beneath the towel before uncinching it from his waist and laying it across the back of a chair.

There. That was better. At least he was covered now. "The shirt is yours. The pants my brother left here when he babysat Emma."

His brow scrunched as he ran his hands down his chest, examining the shirt. "I gave this to you."

She moved toward him. "You said it was so I—"

"Wouldn't forget about me while I was away." He looked into her eyes, and she drifted closer to him, like metal to a magnet...or a mosquito to a bug zapper.

Be careful. You don't know what he's gotten into. "Where did you go that night?"

He paused, his eyes searching hers as if he could find the answer inside her. "I don't know. I can't remember anything unless it involves you."

She took his hand and ran her thumb across the bracelet on his wrist. "I gave this to you. It's a clarity bracelet, so that might be why." She sucked in a sharp breath. "Rain can help. My sister-in-law is a powerful witch. I bet she can write a spell to undo whatever was done to you."

He laced his fingers through hers and kissed the back of her hand. "Do you think it will be that easy?"

Her stomach fluttered. "Witchcraft is never easy, but it's worth a shot. I think I might know how to get in touch with your band. Maybe they can shed some light on what happened."

He rubbed his forehead. "I wish I could remember. I don't recall being in a band." A rumbling sounded from his stomach.

"You must be starving. When was the last time you ate?"

He lifted his hands palms up. "I don't even know where I slept last night."

Poor thing. Her heart ached for him, and the desire to take him in her arms and kiss away the pain surge through her again. "Sit down. I'll get you something to eat."

She could handle this situation if she kept herself busy. Focus on one thing at a time, and she could get through it. This was how she got through college and opened a café while raising her daughter. Tackle the issues as they come and don't get overwhelmed with the big picture.

Of course, the big picture here was that her heart was bound to a man she hardly knew. She gripped the fridge door and blew out a hard breath. *I can handle this.*

She fixed him a turkey sandwich and set it in front of him before retrieving his clothes from the dryer. When she returned to the kitchen, he'd already finished the food, and she handed him his pants. "Go get dressed. The first thing we need to do is get you registered. You're on Crescent City territory, and we don't want to start any issues between the packs."

He wrapped his strong arms around her, pulling her to his chest. "Thank you, Bekah. For everything."

The mix of her soap and his own woodsy scent filled her senses, and she couldn't help but melt into his embrace. There was no doubt in her mind that she was bound to this man, but she'd have to pick Emma up from school soon. She had to figure out a way to keep her family safe and hope her daughter would be okay with having a new person in their lives.

She cleared her throat and pulled from his embrace. "Okay. Let's get you taken care of."

CHAPTER SEVEN

SHANE FOUGHT THE URGE TO TAKE BEKAH'S HAND as they strode toward her pack's headquarters, and he focused on the scenery instead. As they crossed the street, the small, brightly-colored cottages gave way to two- and three-story buildings in shades of beige, yellow, and blue. Potted plants adorned the wrought-iron-trimmed galleries, and colorful beads and purple-and-green wreaths added to the embellishments.

She followed his gaze toward a lavishly decorated balcony. "It'll be Mardi Gras soon."

He smiled, but her lips merely twitched in return. She was holding back, and he honestly couldn't blame her. She had explained the details of their relationship, and as the blanks were filled in, he realized his mistake.

What kind of wanker tells a woman his wolf has claimed her after one date?

The kind who doesn't remember they've only had one date.

He'd overwhelmed her, and he was lucky she'd offered to help him at all. As much as he needed to take her in his arms and make the woman his, he'd dial it back. Give her time to process. Her wolf was dormant, so she might not even feel the strong connection tethering his heart to hers.

She would eventually, and he could wait.

"This is it." She pointed to a dark blue building nestled between two taller structures. A wooden sign above the door read O'Malley's Pub, and a curtain of cool air blasted his skin from above as he followed her inside.

Shaded lights hung from exposed wood beams, and a woman with light-brown hair and bright blue eyes stood behind the bar. She slid the drink she was mixing to a patron and nodded a hello. "Luke and Chase are in the office waiting for you. Head on back."

"Thanks, Amber." Bekah motioned for him to follow and padded toward a side door that had a cardboard sign with *Employees and Werewolves Only* written in black marker.

Shane paused and scratched his head. He may not remember much about his own life, but there was no way the existence of werewolves was out in the open, even in New Orleans. "Is this...?"

Bekah stepped through the door and held it open. "It's a joke. Human customers used to say the old alpha looked like a wolfman, so he went with it."

"I see. What happened to him?" He followed her down a short set of stone steps and through the brick-lined corridor, wracking his brain for a memory of his own alpha—or at least his pack or his family. He found nothing but a void where his memories should have been.

She paused outside an office door and squeezed his hand. "He retired, and his son took over. We're a peaceful pack. Don't worry."

Another sliver of memory from his night with Bekah crept into his mind. "And your brother is his second?"

Her eyes brightened with her smile. "You're remembering."

"Only because it has to do with you."

"It's a start." She dropped his hand and smoothed her hair from her face before knocking on the door.

"It's open," a man called from inside.

Shane straightened his spine and strode through the door, refusing to let the alpha see how lost he felt. A dark-haired man with tattoos and a beard leaned against the massive oak desk, and as Shane stepped through the door, another man rose to his feet and stepped around toward him. This guy was taller, with a barrel of a chest and light-brown hair tied back in a band.

Shane instinctively lowered his gaze, his wolf recognizing the alpha before the man even spoke.

"Hey, guys. This is Shane." Bekah lightly touched his back, ushering him farther into the room. "This is my brother, Chase, and the alpha, Luke."

Shane shook Luke's hand, and the alpha's intense power rolled through his skin. "Pleasure to meet you." He shook Chase's hand, and the man narrowed his eyes, cutting his gaze between Shane and Bekah.

Bekah cleared her throat and settled into a chair, patting the one next to her, indicating Shane should sit too. He reluctantly lowered into the seat, his wolf protesting the submissive position.

Luke strode around his desk and opened a laptop before addressing Bekah. "Chase explained what you told him on the phone, but I need you to go over it again. What's going on?"

"Shane's memory has been wiped. All we know is that he's a British musician who lives in Florida and plays in a local band. He's lived in the States for five years, but he doesn't remember what pack he belongs to or why anyone would do this to him."

The alpha focused on Shane. "How did you end up here?"

He bristled, his body involuntarily reacting to the dominant wolf. "I have no idea how I got here, but I'm positive I came looking for Bekah."

Chase crossed his arms. "Why would you be looking for Bekah?"

She straightened. "He had my clarity bracelet on. Rain's magic probably led him here."

Her brother scowled. "Why did he have your bracelet?"

Pressing her lips together, she flashed Shane an apologetic look. "Now isn't the time to play protective older brother, Chase. I gave it to him, and that's all you need to know."

Shane's chest tightened. He shouldn't have been surprised she didn't want her family to know he'd claimed her. He'd sprung it on her without giving her a chance to get to know him. To fall in love with him. It was wrong of him to expect her to be certain of him the way he was of her.

"That must be what it was." He looked at Chase and then Luke. "This bracelet must be the only thing keeping me grounded, and since it was a gift from Bekah, my subconscious brought me here."

Luke nodded, seemingly satisfied with his answer. "And you have no idea who would have done this to you? Did you get into trouble with a neighboring pack?"

"I honestly have no clue. Bekah said a witch named Rain might be able to help."

Chase stiffened. "You're not bringing my mate into this. This whole situation smells like trouble, and that's the last thing our pack needs."

"I've already called her." Bekah's tone was indignant. "We're heading to the bakery as soon as we're done here."

Chase glared at his sister, and she returned his challenging stare.

"Well?" She crossed her arms to mirror his posture. "Are we done here?"

"You're done. I've still got a few words for your friend."

She dropped her arms by her sides and looked at the alpha. "I can help him, Luke. I think I can get in contact with someone who knows his band. They might be able to fill in the missing pieces of his memory…at least point us to his pack."

Luke shook his head. "It's too dangerous. If whoever did this to him finds out he's here, they might turn on us for harboring him. You can talk to Rain, but don't try to contact anyone he knows. I won't put my pack in harm's way for an outsider."

She lowered her gaze, clasping her hands over her heart. "I understand. The pack comes first. Are we dismissed?"

"Let me know what you find out."

Shane stood and turned to follow Bekah out the door, but Chase put a heavy hand on his shoulder. "A word."

He fought the urge to shrug off Chase's hand, and he touched Bekah on the elbow. "I'll just be a minute."

She nodded, a look of wariness pinching her brow as she shuffled toward the bar.

Chase rubbed at his beard. "I don't know what's going on between you and my sister, but you need to watch yourself."

"I would never do anything to put her in danger." Hell, he'd sacrifice his life for her.

"You being here puts her in danger. She's got a kid, too, and—"

"Emma. She's eight years old. I know." The memory of when Bekah told him skittered through his mind. She'd been afraid he'd lose interest if his lineage were threatened, but he didn't give a damn about lineage. There was a reason he didn't care. Pack status didn't matter either. In fact, having to answer to this alpha and his second sat sour in his stomach like expired milk.

Chase blinked the surprise from his expression. "She's a special little girl, and if anything were to happen to her, your ass would be mine."

"Enough." The alpha's commanding tone put his second in his place.

Chase's posture relaxed, and he took a step back. "If you care about them, you'll leave town. Solve your problems on your own and leave them out of it. They've been through enough already."

The alpha didn't contradict him. "If you do stay in town, keep me posted on your situation. The safety of my pack is my number one priority."

"Understood." Shane strode out the door and shut it behind him.

Bloody hell, Chase was right. Whatever had happened to him, putting his fate-bound in danger was the last thing he wanted to do. He should leave. He could head back to Florida and hope something there would jog his memory. If Bekah could put him in touch with his bandmates, maybe they could help. He could fix his situation and return when he could ensure Bekah's safety… Assuming this ordeal *could* be fixed.

If he couldn't extinguish the threat—whatever it was—he couldn't come back. Ever. The mere thought of never looking into his fate-bound's bright, hazel eyes again tore a gaping hole in his heart.

He paused in the hallway, rubbing his chest. Life without Bekah would be torturous, but he would endure a mountain of suffering to guarantee her safety.

Squaring his shoulders, he paced into the bar and found Bekah sitting on a stool, waiting for him.

"What did my brother say?"

"He said I should leave town. My being here is putting you and your daughter in danger, and he's right. I should go."

"What?" Her eyes widened. "No, Shane, I can help you. We'll figure this out together."

"Bekah." He took her shoulders in his hands. "The last thing I want to do is endanger you or your family. I have a feeling I've been doing things on my own for a while, so let me fix this, and I'll come back to you. I promise."

"No. Absolutely not. Sit your ass on that chair and wait. I'm going to talk to my brother, and when I get done, we are going to see Rain."

"Bekah…"

"No, Shane. You found your way to me. I'm not losing you again. Stay put." She jabbed a finger at him before spinning around and marching through the door.

———

Leave town? These men were insane if they thought she was going to watch her fate-bound walk away. Her hurried strides slowed as her emotions sank in. She'd been hesitant before they'd come here, worrying about what trouble his predicament might bring.

But the thought of him leaving, of having to face this on his own, tore a hole in her chest big enough to swallow her entire world. Meeting Shane when she did was no accident. Fate didn't make mistakes.

He'd found his way to her because he needed her, and she'd be damned if she was going to let anyone take him away.

She stopped herself from shoving the door open. If her brother had been in the office alone, she'd have barged right in, but she knew better than to disrespect

Luke. She knocked, and as Chase opened it, she grabbed his arm and yanked him into the hallway.

"You told him to leave?" Her teeth made an audible click as she clenched her jaw. "Why would you do that?"

He narrowed his eyes. "Your life's not worth risking over some guy you met at a bar." He gripped her shoulder, softening his gaze. "It's better if he goes. If not for your sake, then for Emma's."

She fisted her hands by her sides to stop them from trembling. "If he were *some guy* I met at a bar, I would agree, but he's not." She inclined her chin. "I'm his fate-bound."

Her brother's eyes widened, his mouth dropping open as he gaped at her. "He… How…? He has no memory. How can you be his fate-bound?"

"His memory was fine when I met him. I felt it in him when it happened, and I feel it in him now. That's why he came to New Orleans. He's lost everything, but he managed to find me, and I am not letting him go. If you don't want to help him, that's fine, but Rain has already agreed."

"Why didn't he say so when we questioned him?"

She crossed her arms. "He was respectful to the alpha, and you were looming over him, playing the overprotective big brother and threatening him."

His mouth opened and closed a few times before he spoke. "I was not threatening him."

"Yes, you were, and you owe him an apology."

"I'm sorry, Bekah. If I'd known…"

"Well, now you do, so make it right. He's here to stay." She stormed through the door into the bar, and her heart dropped when she spied the empty seat where Shane had been.

Amber raised her hands. "I tried to get him to stay, but he insisted he had to take care of it on his own."

"Christ. Where does he think he's going to go?" She darted out of the bar, stopping on the sidewalk and looking right and left. Instinct pulled her right, and she rounded the corner to find Shane leaning against the wall, pinching the bridge of his nose as he squeezed his eyes shut.

She ran to him, taking his shoulders in her hands. "What are you doing?"

"I want to fix this. I thought I could go to Florida, but I don't have a car. I don't have any money… I have nothing."

The pain in his eyes shattered her heart, and she wrapped her arms around him. As he slid his arms to her waist, she cupped his face in her hands, pressing her lips to his. He opened for her, deepening the kiss as he tightened his embrace. She fit in his arms like she was made for him to hold, and she refused to fight the magnetic pull his wolf had on her. Fate had a plan for them, and she was ready to follow it.

As the kiss slowed, she touched her forehead to his. "You have me, Shane."

"You have us." Chase stepped toward them, and though skepticism tightened his eyes, he offered his hand to Shane. "You should have told me she was your fate-bound."

Shane accepted the handshake. "I didn't know it would make a difference."

"It makes all the difference. You're with my sister, you're one of us. Let's go see Rain."

Bekah rested her head on Shane's shoulder and smiled at her brother. Chase had been willing to run to hell and back when his fate-bound was in trouble. He understood the bond of fated mates, even as she was still adjusting to it.

CHAPTER EIGHT

Shane held Bekah's hand as they paced down Royal Street toward a bright-yellow building. Tourists meandered along the sidewalk, pausing to look into the shop windows, and the mid-afternoon sun hung high in the sky, warming his face like the woman next to him warmed his soul.

A deep sense of gratitude settled in his heart. The way Bekah, and now her brother and his mate, had dropped everything to help him felt foreign, and he couldn't tell if it was because *everything* felt new to him or if he'd never had this kind of support before.

He gazed up at the nineteenth-century buildings —old structures by American standards—their decorative wrought-iron railings swirling across the galleries lined with ferns, and he smiled. He could get used to living in this city.

A bell chimed as Chase opened a wooden door, and the scents of cinnamon and vanilla wafted to Shane's senses as he entered Spellbound Sweets bakery. To his left stood a glass case filled with cookies and other delicacies, and two women laughed behind the counter.

The tall, platinum blonde lifted a hand to wave. "Hey, guys." She looked at Shane. "I'm Snow."

He nodded. "Nice to meet you."

The other woman, with long, dark curls and stormy gray eyes, shuffled around the counter and stepped into Chase's arms, placing a kiss on his lips. "I didn't expect you to come. Is everything okay?"

Chase brushed a curl from her face, his love for his mate evident in his eyes. "It seems my sister has bonded with a Brit. It's pack business now."

Bekah squeezed Shane's hand before releasing it and sliding an arm around his waist. Damn, it felt good for her to touch him, to slip into his embrace like they'd been together their entire lives. "This is Shane." She paused and looked into his eyes. "My fate-bound."

Her lips curled into a smile as she said it, and his heart pounded harder. Maybe he didn't need his memory back. Whatever happened to him between his life in London and finding his way here didn't matter as long as he had Bekah by his side.

He shook Rain's hand, and her magical signature buzzed across his skin, revealing her immense power.

She pursed her lips and studied him, her gaze shifting to the area around him. "His powers aren't bound, which is a good thing. Unbinding spells are a bitch. But there's a current of dark magic running through his aura. He's definitely been cursed."

Bekah's arm tightened around him, and his heart sank. Whatever trouble he'd gotten into, he didn't want to bring it to New Orleans...to Bekah. "Can you break the curse?"

"Come back to the kitchen, and I'll mix something up." Rain padded around the counter, and he followed, slipping his hand into Bekah's as she released her hold of his waist.

Stainless steel countertops gleamed in the overhead lights, and the heat from an oven warmed the space as he stepped deeper into the room. A fresh batch of cookies sat on a cooling rack, and Rain pulled a chocolate cake from the oven before dropping her mitts and standing in front of him.

She placed her hands on either side of his head, closing her eyes and swaying slightly. She shivered and dropped her arms. "Black magic. Whoever did this to you was incredibly powerful, but I can undo it. The spell will take time to work, though."

"How much time, *cher*?" Chase grabbed a cookie from the rack. "We have no idea what kind of danger he's in."

Rain gathered herbs from a cabinet, dumping them into a bowl and grinding them with a pestle, wafting the savory scent of rosemary into the air. "Could be a few days. Maybe a week."

That was a long time to go without his memory. Without anything. He could play his sax on the street for money. The tourists had dropped seven dollars in his case for the one song he'd played outside Bekah's café. He could shift and sleep in the woods until he earned enough for a room.

"Emma can stay with us." Chase's voice pulled him from his thoughts. "And we'll patrol your house to make sure nothing tries to sneak in while he's recovering."

"I don't think we need the patrol, but I agree about Emma…just to be safe." Bekah flashed him a small smile.

They were talking like he was part of their pack. As if there were no question where he would stay or how he'd get along while he waited for the spell to break. Gratitude ballooned in his chest again, along with a sense of disbelief, making him wonder how his trust had been damaged before. That was something he'd rather not remember.

"I'm sure I'll be fine on my own. I apparently made it three days and several hundred miles with no memory. No need to worry about me."

Bekah looked at him as if he were crazy. "You're staying with me."

Chase nodded. "We take care of our own."

Their own. As if Shane were one of them. A memory buzzed in the back of his mind, and a feeling of abandonment attempted to form. But it flitted away the moment he tried to bring it into focus.

"Here, drink this." Rain handed him a cup of bright-blue liquid.

Little flecks of silver sparkled in the mixture, and he hesitated, casting a glance at Bekah.

"It's safe." She smiled and nodded, gesturing for him to drink.

He swallowed the liquid, and a sweet, bubblegum flavor filled his mouth as a cooling sensation crept down his throat.

Rain took the glass, setting it on the counter. "Is that Bekah's clarity bracelet?"

"It is."

"May I?" She held out her hand, so he slipped off the bracelet and gave it to her. Holding it between her palms, she whispered a spell before carrying it to her cupboard and sprinkling it with herbs. "Here you go." She handed it back to him, and he put it on. "I recharged the clarity spell. It should help the potion bring your memories back, so keep it on at all times."

"Thanks, Rain." Bekah took Shane's hand before looking at her brother. "Will you pick Emma up from school? I'll pack a bag for her, and you can pick it up on your way."

Chase glanced between them. "I think Emma should meet him."

"Maybe better to wait until we figure out what happened," Bekah said.

"Emma is intuitive. She might be able to give us a new perspective on the situation." He cleared his throat. "Not that I don't believe you two are fate-bound, but...he's under a spell, and you've been wrong before."

Rain put her hand on Chase's shoulder. "I don't—"

"Emma was right about us before I even figured it out." Chase arched an eyebrow at his mate. "It can't hurt."

A look passed between the three of them, and

Shane tempered his curiosity. Something had happened in the past for this cryptic conversation to make sense to everyone except him, but he'd wait until he had Bekah alone to ask for an explanation.

"Y'all head home," Chase said, "and I'll swing by with Emma as soon as school lets out."

Bekah sat on the couch next to Shane and fired up her laptop. "Your band's name had witch in the title. Witch Ways or something like that. We can probably do a Google search to figure out who they are."

She opened a web browser and glanced at Shane. "I met a witch at the conference named Tambra, and her cousin is the drummer. Blonde hair, blue eyes? Does any of this ring a bell?"

He rubbed his forehead as if searching for the memories pained him. "Not a bit of it."

She put her hand on his knee, and he immediately covered it with his own. "Rain said it will take a few days. We'll do some research in the meantime and see if we can at least figure out your last name."

Shane chuckled. "We probably should have exchanged full names before hopping into bed. I can't say for sure, but it doesn't feel like that's the kind of thing I normally do."

"I've never done anything like that, but it doesn't matter. If we really are fate-bound…"

"What do you mean *if?*"

She lowered her gaze, chewing her bottom lip as her brother's words rolled through her mind. *He's under a spell, and you've been wrong before.*

"Bekah?" He cupped her cheek in his hand, turning her head toward him to catch her gaze. "Are you having doubts? Does this have anything to do with what Chase said?"

She licked her lips, unable to force the words from her throat. *What if I'm wrong again?*

"Have you thought someone's wolf claimed you before?" The hurt in his eyes tugged at her heart.

"No. He was talking about Emma's father. When Tommy left, I should have seen it coming. My ability, since I'm second-born, is empathy. When I touch people, I can feel their emotions. I should have felt Tommy recoiling when he found out I was pregnant, but my own emotions overpowered my ability."

She laced her fingers through his, opening her senses to Shane's emotions. So many feelings swirled through him it was a wonder he could sit upright, but the same strong undercurrent provided a foundation to it all. His wolf wanted her...unless the emotions were fabricated with a spell.

"I felt your wolf claim me the night we met, but when you stood me up, I assumed it had been wishful thinking on my part. But I felt it again this morning outside the café, and I still feel it in you now."

"What's the problem then? I know it happened fast, but that's the nature of fate."

She set the computer on the coffee table and turned to face him. "Before Rain met Chase, she was under a spell that made her think she was in love with someone. It had a messy, bloody ending, and I worry...with the spell that wiped your memory...what if that's not the only spell you're under?"

He took both her hands in his. "I wasn't under a spell the night we met, love, and that's when my wolf claimed you. This is real."

"What if it isn't? You were in a band of witches. One of them could have..."

He laughed. "I hope I'm smart enough not to associate with people who would put a spell on me."

"Maybe someone they know did it. I don't know, Shane, but I've been burned before." Emma had never met her father, but she was about to meet Shane. What if she bonded with him, and once the spells cleared, he left? She couldn't put her daughter through that.

"I understand, but I also know what I feel in my soul, and we belong to each other. What can I do to prove it to you?"

"Let's give it some time. See what happens when your memories return before we start planning a mating ceremony." It was the logical thing to do. Every fiber of her being may have been telling her to make the man hers, but like Chase said...she'd been wrong before.

Shane brought her fingers to his lips and kissed them. "Take all the time you need, love. I'm not going anywhere without you."

A knock sounded on the door, and she shot to her feet, thankful for the distraction from Shane's intense gaze. "That'll be Emma." A glance through the peephole confirmed her daughter was home, so she threw open the door and scooped the little girl into her arms. "Hi, sweetheart. How was your day?"

Emma gave her neck a squeeze before wiggling from her embrace. "Good. Is this Shane?" She narrowed her eyes at him as Chase slipped in behind her.

"Be polite, Emma," Bekah said. "Say 'hello.'"

"Hi. Uncle Chase is skepi...skept...ical of you."

She stepped in front of him, assessing him with her gaze.

At eight years old, Emma hadn't fully come into her powers yet, but she had an uncanny ability to detect relationships between people. She was also an excellent judge of character.

"I'd be concerned if he wasn't." Shane smiled, holding out his hand to shake, and Emma accepted. "Hello, Emma. It's nice to meet you."

She gripped his hand, holding on longer than politely necessary, studying him. With a deep inhale, she cut her gaze between Shane and Bekah before looking over her shoulder at her uncle. "He's cool."

"That's good to know." The tension in Chase's shoulders eased, and Bekah's own posture relaxed with her daughter's confirmation.

With her free hand, Emma took her mom's hand, holding onto both Bekah and Shane for a moment before placing Bekah's hand in his and stepping back. "I approve." She strolled to the recliner and grabbed the overnight bag Bekah had packed for her.

Slinging it over her shoulder, she paused and eyed Shane's saxophone case sitting by the couch. "What's that?"

His eyes brightened. "It's my saxophone. Would

you like to see it?" Shane dropped to his knees and opened the case, offering the instrument to Emma.

Bekah's throat thickened as her daughter moved toward him, running her hand along the brass. The smile lighting up Emma's face made her heart ache.

"Will you teach me to play it?"

Shane grinned, returning the instrument to its case. "I would love to." He tapped his temple. "As soon as my mind is working right, yeah?"

"I hope you're better soon." Emma shuffled to the door and took Chase's hand. "When his memory comes back, will we be moving to England, or will he live here?"

Bekah blinked, her daughter's words wrapping around her heart and squeezing it tight. While her own emotions could hinder her ability, she'd never known Emma to be wrong about anyone.

"I'm never going back to England." Shane's brow shot up as if he'd surprised himself with the declaration.

"Was that a memory?" She squeezed his hand, fighting the urge to throw her arms around him.

He blinked a few times, his mouth screwing up to the side as he searched his mind. "More like a feeling."

"It's a start."

"It certainly is."

She squatted to eye-level with Emma and put her hands on her shoulders. "You'll be okay spending a few days with Aunt Rain and Uncle Chase? It's just until we know you'll be safe."

Emma smiled. "Aunt Rain's going to make chocolate muffins for breakfast every morning, and Uncle Chase promised to take me to the park this weekend."

"Sounds like you're going to have a great time. I'll see you soon." She hugged her daughter, and they said their goodbyes. As Chase led Emma down the front steps, Bekah turned to Shane.

God, he was a beautiful man, with his chiseled features and soulful eyes. She couldn't stop herself from stepping into his inviting embrace, and as the protective cage of his arms closed around her, she wanted nothing more than to give herself to him. To feel his hands on her body, his lips setting fire to her skin.

But if Rain, the most powerful witch she'd ever met, could be fooled by a spell, it was possible Emma's judgment could be clouded too. Unlikely, but the possibility remained, so she would keep her guard up, at least for a little while.

CHAPTER NINE

Over the next week, Bekah spent every spare moment she had helping Shane recover his memory. Through her Internet searches, she discovered his band and found their Facebook page. Photos of Shane playing and lounging with the members should have jogged his mind, but he couldn't recall a single moment with any of them.

Bekah cleared the dishes from a café table, handing the tray to a waitress on her way to the kitchen. At least some of Shane's other memories were returning. The process seemed painful for him, but reversing black magic was never easy.

The music had never left him, though. With the patio doors wide open, Bekah stood in her café watching Shane play his saxophone for the customers outside. He'd been nervous at first, but he borrowed her phone to look up the requested songs he couldn't remember, and as soon as he heard the tune, his fingers flew across the keys like the song had been ingrained in his being.

He spent the days entertaining the patrons while Bekah worked in the café, and when she had lunch with Emma at school each afternoon, he wandered the French Quarter, familiarizing himself with the city. It was a routine she could get used to.

As he finished his instrumental rendition of "Shape of You" by Ed Sheeran, he glanced inside and caught her gaze. With a wink, he started "Careless Whisper," and the familiar hummingbirds took flight in her stomach as her lips curved into a goofy grin. She could never get enough of this man.

Dani stepped out of the kitchen, tying an apron around her waist, and picked up a serving tray. "Jeez. I go visit family for a few days, and when I come back to work, Hottie Homeless Guy is now our live entertainment. What did I miss?"

Bekah tore her gaze away from Shane's sexy mouth caressing the sax and tucked a strand of hair behind her ear. "His name is Shane, and I know him. We had a misunderstanding before, but we've worked it out." Her gaze drifted back to the patio.

"So, he's here to stay? You two are…"

"He's a great guy." And she was an idiot for insisting they keep their distance from each other. His memories were slowly coming back. He could recall his family now, and he remembered his mom teaching him the love of music. In fact, the more he played, the more he seemed to remember.

And while his confusion was clearing, his emotions stabilizing, the solid sentiment that fate had bound their hearts was unwavering. If his feelings for her were fabricated by a spell, it would have cracked by now, wouldn't it? It was time she consulted a witch to be sure.

Dani held the tray to her chest and drummed her nails on it. "He's a great guy and a talented musician, but are you shacking up?" She wiggled her eyebrows. "Is he your beau?"

Bekah grinned. "If I say yes, will you get to work and wait on some customers?"

The waitress nodded.

"Yes. We're a couple. Now go." She pointed to the dining room. "I have to make a phone call."

"I'll keep an eye on him for you." Dani winked and sashayed toward a table.

Bekah ducked into the office and dialed Rain's number on the office phone. Her sister-in-law picked up on the third ring. "Thank you for calling Spell-bound Sweets. This is Rain. How can I help you?"

"Is it possible this fate-bound thing is because of the spell Shane is under?"

Shuffling sounded in the receiver as the background noise quieted. "There's not a spell in existence that can mimic the werewolf mating bond. That's something that runs soul-deep, and if you'll stop second-guessing yourself, you'll realize that. Even Emma sees it."

She chewed her lip, trying desperately to rid her mind of the doubt. "But if it were a spell, couldn't it fool Emma too? You were fooled."

Rain let out a heavy sigh. "That was different. Isaac wasn't a werewolf, and what I thought I felt for him was a speck of dust. Chase is my whole world. I know it's scary, but you've got the real deal with Shane. That potion I gave him was an all-inclusive banishing spell. The only curse I sensed in him was the memory wipe, but if he was being affected by anything else, it's gone now."

"Are you sure?" Of course Rain was sure. Bekah was sure deep in her soul. She was letting her thoughts consume her, hold her back from her fate.

"I'm positive, but I can come by and have another look at him if you want. His aura was strong, though.

If his memories are returning, and you still feel the bond, it's safe to say he's yours."

"Thanks, Rain. You're the best." Her chest expanded like a can of store-bought biscuits popping open in her heart. She hung up the phone and grabbed her purse from the drawer.

Whatever danger he was in, they would face it together, because together was where they belonged. She was done holding back with Shane, and he was done sleeping on the couch.

Shane sat on Bekah's sofa, staring at the picture of him and his bandmates on her laptop screen. Over the past week, the potion Rain gave him had knocked loose most of his memories. They came in chunks, mostly returning while he was playing his sax, which made sense now that he remembered his history with his mum and how much music had meant to him throughout his life.

He blew out a hard breath and closed the computer. When it came to his most recent band, he couldn't remember a bloody thing. Their faces weren't familiar. He couldn't recall what kind of music they played. Hell, he wouldn't believe they existed at all if Bekah hadn't seen him play with them.

He could see in his mind the night he played "Careless Whisper" for Bekah. Could see her sweet smile and the spark of lust in her eyes as she watched him. But as he tried to expand his vision, to see where he was or who was around him, he saw nothing but inky blackness.

The band had to be involved in his curse, but he couldn't fathom a reason why.

His life before the curse grew clearer by the hour. His night with Bekah was as vivid in his mind as if it happened yesterday. But the days…or possibly years…leading up to the moment he met her were empty.

He remembered his girlfriend dumping him in Florida. The feelings of betrayal gnawed in his gut, but he also remembered not being surprised when it happened. He'd been on his own most of his life, and his father had taught him from a young age that he couldn't depend on anyone…and that no one should rely on him.

He'd been raised a rogue, his dad insisting packs existed to control people. That werewolves were better off on their own, and no one could be trusted. The old man had proven that himself when he told Shane if he chose music, not to come back to London.

Raking a hand through his hair, he watched the beautiful woman putting away the dishes in the kitchen. He'd offered to help, but she'd insisted he sit down and rest, his quietness at dinner making her worry…about *him*.

He could depend on Bekah. She'd proven herself again and again, not that she'd needed to. His wolf knew, and that was good enough for him. Her pack was nothing like what his father had claimed. They treated him like he belonged.

Shane had never belonged anywhere.

"Almost done. You okay?" Bekah raised her brows as she gazed at him from the kitchen, her hazel eyes holding more concern than he was used to seeing. She cared deeply for him, but how would she feel when he told her he was a rogue?

"Fine, love. No rush."

Bekah's brother was second in command, which gave her pack status. When she'd talked casually about Shane's past, she'd assumed he was in a pack too. She might revolt at the idea of mating with a man who'd grown up a rogue. Her pack might not even allow them to be mates.

His stomach turned at the idea of losing her over a past he'd have been fine not remembering.

She smiled as she shuffled into the living room and sank onto the sofa next to him. Resting her hand on his knee, she pressed a kiss to his temple, and his chest gave a squeeze. "You remembered a lot today, didn't you? Too much to process?"

This woman could read him like a book. Even when she wasn't using her empathic powers, she seemed to sense his moods. "Quite a bit, yeah."

"Anything you want to talk about?"

All of it. None of it. If he could, he'd whisk her away in the night. Take her and Emma to Australia or somewhere far away from whatever trouble he was in. But Bekah was rooted in this pack. Her daughter had friends here. If he wanted to be with her, he had to face it all. No running this time.

"I still don't remember the band. It's like they don't exist, and those photos are fabricated."

Bekah nodded. "They're all witches, but who knows if any of them are powerful enough to do this to you. It would be a lot easier if we could contact them, but Luke forbade it." She squeezed his knee and folded her hands in her lap. "We have a meeting with him tomorrow to talk about what you remember, and maybe he'll let us contact them then."

His father's words rang in his mind. *Packs exist to control.*

Maybe. Or perhaps their purpose was to protect. "I understand his reasoning. If the band is responsible…" He rubbed his forehead. Forcing the memories made his head ache.

Bekah took his hand. "We'll figure it out. In the meantime, I wanted to talk to you about something."

"There's something else I need to tell you too." And the sooner he got it off his chest, the better. He couldn't hide it from her.

"Just let me say this, okay? I think it will help you feel better."

He clamped his mouth shut and nodded.

"I've been holding back because I've been scared. I feel the mating bond with you…in my own heart and in yours, but my brother…" She huffed. "Chase is skeptical of everyone at first, and I let his ideas burrow into my brain, even though I know better. I *know* this bond we share is real, and I'm sorry for doubting you. I want to be with you, Shane, and from this point forward, I'm all in."

"Oh, Bekah." He leaned back on the couch and squeezed his eyes shut. Her words coiled around his heart, squeezing it until he thought it would burst. It was precisely what he wanted to hear, but she didn't know his past. He'd lured her in under false pretenses, assuming he'd been a pack man because she wanted him to be.

"That's not the reaction I was expecting." She tucked her hair behind her ears. "What's going on? You've been quiet since we got home."

There was no use in sugar-coating it. He just needed to tell her. *Well, go on then, mate. Spit it out.* Opening his eyes, he turned to look at her. "I'm a rogue. I always have been." He braced himself for her recoil, but she didn't even flinch.

"Okay?" An amused grin curved her lips. "Is that what's been bothering you all evening? You remembered you're a rogue, and you thought I would object?"

"Well, yeah. You're an integral part of your pack. Your whole family is. I'll bring shame to your bloodline."

She laughed a deep, musical belly laugh. "Shane…" She sucked in a breath and clutched his hands, attempting to get her amusement under control. "My parents were rogues. My dad died when I was little, and my mom joined this pack because my brother was so wild she couldn't handle him. I got pregnant when I was nineteen by a man who never wanted to be my mate, and the only reason my brother has the status he does is that his best friend is the alpha."

She scooted closer to him, wrapping her arms around his shoulders and kissing his cheek. "And after all that, we've never been shamed. This is a good, peaceful pack. We take care of our own, and we leave no one behind."

Leaning back, she looked into his eyes. "The only problem that could come from you being a rogue is if you intend to stay that way. Are you willing to settle down and join us? Sleep in the same bed every night?"

Settle down. Stay in one place. It was exactly what he wanted. Being part of a pack would take some getting used to, but he was up for the challenge. "Bekah, as long as that bed has you in it, I will gladly settle down."

"That can be arranged." She held his gaze, the green and gold in her hazel irises shimmering with her smile. "We'll figure out everything about your missing memories tomorrow. Tonight, I want to be with you."

She leaned into him, taking his mouth in a kiss as she pushed him onto his back. With his head resting on the arm of the sofa, he held her tight, parting his lips and dipping his tongue into her warm, sweet mouth.

Slipping her hand beneath his shirt, she ran her palm up his stomach, gripping his chest as a moan vibrated across her lips. She broke the kiss to sit up, tugging his shirt over his head and tossing it to the floor before removing her own.

With a fire in her eyes that set his soul ablaze, she dragged her hands down his chest, her tongue slipping out to moisten her lips as she popped the button on his jeans and tugged at the zipper. She worked the fabric over his hips, rising to her feet to pull his clothes from his legs, stepping out of her own pants before diving on top of him and kissing him again.

She was a goddess wrapped in pink satin, and the feel of her supple body pressed to his was enough to drive him mad. He stroked his hands up and down her back, gripping her ass and grinding his hips against hers, her quick intake of breath and the goose bumps running down her arms his reward.

With a mischievous grin, she inched downward, pressing her lips to his neck, grazing his nipples with her teeth, her mouth growing nearer and nearer to his dick. He held his breath as she kissed down to his hip, his stomach tightening as she lifted her head, and her warm breath blew across his cock.

Taking his length in her hand, she stroked it with

her tongue from base to tip, circling around the head and flicking her gaze to his. She watched him intently as she took him into her mouth, sliding up until only the tip remained between her lips.

He groaned, the sensation of being enveloped in warm, wet velvet forcing his lids closed. He wouldn't last long at all like this, so he opened his eyes and put a hand on her head to still her. "I need to be inside you, Bekah. Make love to me."

She smiled wickedly, rising onto her knees and tossing her bra aside before shimmying out of her panties. Straddling him, she used her hand to guide him to her folds, lowering herself onto him slowly, until their bodies joined as one.

He paused, clutching her hips to hold her still and memorizing the way they fit together. "This..." He glided his hands up her sides to cup her breasts. "Is the most beautiful sight I've ever seen."

As he teased her nipples, she slid up and down his dick, the sensuous friction sending an electric current buzzing through his muscles. Her magic mingled with his, dancing across his skin, setting every nerve in his body on fire.

His climax coiled in his core, but there was no way he'd come before she did. He licked his thumb and pressed it to her clit, working the sensitive nub in circles until she cried out, tossing her head back as she rode him through her orgasm.

As her rhythm slowed, he grabbed her ass and flipped her onto her back, never breaking their intimate union as he covered her body with his and took her. He thrust deep inside her, hooking his arms behind her shoulders and burying his face in her neck. He was in her, a part of her, but he still felt like he couldn't get close enough.

She couldn't possibly realize the level of his devotion. He'd stop the world from spinning if she asked him to. "Feel me, Bekah."

"It feels so good, Shane." She clutched his back, wrapping her legs around his waist as he pumped his hips.

"Use your power. Feel what I feel. I want you to know."

She flattened her palms on his back and sucked in a sharp breath. "I feel you." Her whisper against his ear nearly sent him over the edge.

"Do you understand?"

"You belong to me. Like I belong to you."

His orgasm exploded through his body, a rippling wave of ecstasy crashing into him, shattering his senses.

"Oh my God, Shane." Still connected to his

emotions, Bekah rode the crest of his orgasm, her body trembling as if it were her own.

He collapsed on top of her, panting, showering her face and neck in kisses as his heart rate slowed. Still gripping his waist with her legs, she relaxed her arms, sliding her hands to his shoulders as he rose onto his elbows to look at her.

She was a vision of beauty with tousled, dark hair and passion-drunk eyes looking up at him like he was the only man in the world. To him, she was the only woman.

"No more doubts about us, yeah?" He kissed her forehead, her nose, her mouth. "We're meant to be."

She smiled. "No doubts. We're fate-bound."

CHAPTER TEN

BEKAH LAY NESTLED IN THE CROOK OF SHANE'S arm, her head resting on his shoulder. After their intense lovemaking on the couch, they eventually made it to the bedroom, where they did it all over again.

And again.

She couldn't fight her smile. Emma would finally have a full-time father in her life, and Shane seemed excited at the prospect. This afternoon, he'd be joining them at Emma's school for lunch.

With the help of the pack, she had no doubt they'd figure out what happened to Shane's memory. They'd end the threat—whatever it was—and she'd get her happily ever after.

Shane stirred, turning onto his side and pulling her

into his arms. This was exactly where she belonged; all the pieces of her life were finally clicking into place. She snuggled into his chest and breathed in his intoxicating scent, reveling in the protectiveness of his embrace.

With a gasp, he jerked, flopping onto his back and clutching the sheets, dragging the corner off the edge of the bed. She sat up, placing her hand on his shoulder and trying to soothe him, but he squeezed his eyes shut in a pained expression.

"Shane?" She shook him gently. He'd had similar episodes several times during the night, his restless movements rousing Bekah from sleep before he'd roll over and settle down.

This time, his lids flew open, and he gasped, shooting upright and dragging the sheets from the bed. "Oh, God, I remember." He looked at her, eyes wild, and jabbed his fingers into his hair, pulling it at the roots. "I remember everything."

Her phone rang from the nightstand, and she glanced at the screen as the café's landline number lit up the device. She let the call go to voicemail and rubbed Shane's back. "What do you remember?"

He sucked in a shaky breath. "It was Cammie. The drummer. Damn it, and Ricardo helped her. They wanted me out of the way."

"Out of the way of what?" Her phone rang again, and she snatched it from the nightstand, holding up a finger to Shane. "Hello?"

"Bekah, I'm sorry to bother you on your day off," her manager said, "but this woman left eight messages on the recorder before I got in this morning. Someone named Tambra. She sounded frantic, so I thought you might want to know."

"Did she leave a number?" With a trembling hand, she scribbled the digits onto a notepad and ended the call. "Tambra is trying to reach me."

"That's Cammie's cousin. Bloody hell, what did she do?" Shane marched down the hallway and returned with their discarded clothes. He shoved his legs into his jeans and paced in front of the bed.

"What *did* she do, Shane? Why did she wipe your memory?"

He groaned. "A stupid plan. The most idiotic thing she could have done. I wanted nothing to do with it, so they ambushed me." He stopped pacing and dropped his arms to his sides. "Ricardo called me that night in your hotel room. I left you there because he said Cammie was in trouble. I should have known better than to trust them."

"Let me call Tambra and see what's going on."

He sat on the edge of the bed. "Don't tell her I'm with you. Cammie wanted to kill me."

"Jesus, Shane." She dialed the number, and Tambra answered on the second ring.

"Hey, it's Bekah. I got a message that you called."

The sound of a car engine emanated through the headset, and a horn blared in the background. "Are you still seeing Shane? Do you know where he is?"

"What's going on? Why are you breathless?" She put the phone on speaker and held it up so Shane could hear.

"Cammie's dead." Tambra sucked in a breath. "They're all dead, and it's going after the ones they love."

Shane's face paled, his jaw going slack.

"What are you talking about, Tambra? Who's going after them?"

She lowered her voice to a whisper. "They summoned a demon. I told her she was crazy when she told me the plan, but she did it anyway. It's linked to all of them, and Bekah...she completed the spell with werewolf blood. It had to be Shane's. Something went wrong. There was more magic in his blood than she could control, and a demon broke through the veil. They couldn't appease it, so it killed them all. They've found all the bodies, except Shane's."

"Oh my God." Bekah's eyes widened.

Shane shot to his feet, clenching and unclenching his hands.

"If you know where he is, you have to warn him. It's coming for him, and Bekah, if you're with him… it's coming for you too. I got out of town before it could find me, but if someone doesn't stop it…"

Shane threw on the rest of his clothes and stuffed his feet into his boots. He marched toward the front door, and Bekah followed, catching him by the arm before he could open it.

"Why would it be coming for me?"

"It got inside their minds. It killed the other band members and their girlfriends before it came after Cammie and Ricardo. She called me, warned me to get out of town. It's not going to stop until it kills them all and everyone they love."

Shane tried to move toward the door, but she tightened her grip on his arm. "Take care of yourself. If I see Shane, I'll let him know."

"Be careful." Tambra ended the call.

"Where do you think you're going?" Bekah tossed the phone on the coffee table.

"I have to stop it."

"Shane." She clutched his shoulders, staring him hard in the eyes. "It's six o'clock in the morning.

Demons only act at night, and you don't have to face it alone. Let me get dressed, and we'll talk to Luke. The pack will handle it. They'll help you."

Her phone rang again, her brother's name illuminating the screen this time, and she pressed the device to her ear.

"Are y'all safe?"

Her pulse thrummed. "We're okay. What's going on?"

"Two musicians were murdered outside a club on Frenchman around four a.m. It looks demonic," Chase said.

Her blood ran cold. "Shit."

"What do you know?"

"Call Mom and have her take Emma away for a few days. Meet us at the bar, and we'll explain."

"They ambushed me." Shane ground his teeth as he paced in front of the alpha's desk. "My mind was… elsewhere." He glanced at Bekah sitting in a chair, and then at Rain. "They told me they were going to remove me from the spell, but they bound me to it even tighter."

A flush of anger heated his chest. He'd trusted his

bandmates, and now his misjudgment had put Bekah and her pack in danger. He was an idiot.

"Blood magic is tricky." Rain leaned into Chase's side. "If your friends made a blood sacrifice to the demon for his help, adding were blood into the mix would have made the offering volatile at best. If she was powerful enough to paralyze a werewolf, I'm not surprised a fiend was able to escape through the rift she tore in the veil."

"I read the reports from the pack in charge of the area." Luke tapped a few keys on the laptop. "It appears the demon went in through the nasal cavity, accessed their memories, and then scrambled their brains. Aside from a few scrapes and bruises from the struggle, that's the only injury. Same for the two we found on Frenchman last night."

Shane let out his breath in a hiss. "Bastard was recharging, and then the sun came up."

"Probably," Chase said. "He felt the power in your blood and knew you wouldn't be as easy of a target as the others, and with the distance he traveled in one night…he needed an energy boost."

"What's the plan?" Bekah clutched Shane's arm to stop his pacing. "We can sit here and speculate the why and how all day, but what are we going to do to stop it before anyone else gets killed?" She tightened her grip on his arm, her icy fingers digging into his flesh, betraying the fear that her confident voice hid.

The alpha closed his computer and folded his arms on the desk. "Chase, contact James and Cade. Fill them in on the details. We'll need their help."

Chase nodded, and Luke focused on Shane, his heavy gaze making the hairs on the back of his neck stand on end. "You'll be the bait. Before sunset, we'll take you to our hunting grounds, away from the city. The demon will follow, and then we'll attack. I don't care how powerful the fiend is; it won't stand a chance against the five of us."

The five of *us*. The alpha lumped him in with the pack as if he were one of them. From the moment they'd discovered he was bound to Bekah, they'd taken him in, treated him like he belonged.

We take care of our own. He'd heard their mantra several times since he arrived, but he wasn't one of them. Not yet. He couldn't let them risk their lives for the trouble he'd brought to their territory.

He should have left when Chase first told him to. Battled the demon on his own once it found him. Then, if he'd lost the fight, he wouldn't have had any memories for the fiend to use to find his loved ones.

Except for Bekah.

His hands curled into fists. He could slip away

this afternoon and fight the demon by himself, but if he lost… He couldn't take the risk of it coming after Bekah and Emma.

"Right." He nodded at Luke. "That sounds like a plan, then." Not a plan that would ever come to fruition, but he knew better than to try negotiating with an alpha. He'd handle this problem on his own like he'd been doing his entire life. Then, if he survived, he'd find his way back to his fate-bound.

Shane spent the rest of the morning and into the early afternoon holed up in Bekah's house. She made him lunch and tried her best to soothe his frazzled nerves, but his beast couldn't be quieted.

Luke's plan was too risky. Rain was right; if Cammie were powerful enough to paralyze a were-wolf, take his blood, and wipe his memory, she would have been able to defeat any mid to lower-level demon that came after her. Her death meant whatever she'd turned loose was stronger than anything he—or Bekah's pack—had ever dealt with.

If they couldn't defeat it…if it got into his head and went after Bekah…

He couldn't let that happen, and there was only one way he knew to ensure it wouldn't.

Bekah's phone rang, and her entire face lit up as she answered it. "Hey, pumpkin! Did you and grandma make it to Shreveport?"

She paused to let Emma speak, and Shane's chest tightened at the joy in her voice. He was supposed to make their family complete. Damn Cammie and Ricardo...and the whole bloody band for messing with his fate.

"You have fun, and I'll see you in a couple of days. Oh, okay." She held the phone toward him. "She wants to talk to you."

His heart racing, he took the device and pressed it to his ear. "Hey, Emma. How are you?"

"My mom loves you, and I know you love her too." She said it like it was a matter of fact, the most obvious thing in the world. "So take care of her while I'm gone, okay?"

He swallowed the lump from his throat. "Yeah. Of course. Everything's going to be fine."

"And when I get back, you'll be safe, right? And we can all be a family?"

"Umm... How do you know we'll be a family? Did your mum tell you that?" He glanced at Bekah, and she smiled, shaking her head.

Emma sighed. "A girl just knows these things. I don't know why I have to keep telling people that. You can't fight fate."

"You're right. No one can." It was his fate to be a part of this family, and he would do everything he could to fix what Cammie broke. "I'll see you soon."

"Bye, Shane." Emma ended the call, and he handed the phone to Bekah.

"I told you she's intuitive," Bekah said.

"She's a special girl." He pulled her into a hug, pressing his lips to her temple, closing his eyes and memorizing the way she felt in his arms.

This would not be the last time he held her. If he found her before, he could do it again. "I'm going to go for a walk, yeah? I need to get out of the house and clear my head before tonight."

"I can imagine you must be getting cabin fever. Do you want me to come with you?" She held his gaze, and his will nearly crumbled. But he had to do this. It was the only way.

"Give me a little time. I just…need to be alone for a bit. It's a lot to process."

"Promise you'll come back to me?" She said it in a joking way, but uneasiness underscored her humor.

"Always." He picked up his sax case, and she gave him a curious look.

"You are coming back, right?" She glanced at the case, concern creasing her forehead. "You're not taking your most prized possession with you because you're planning on running away, are you?"

"Music helps me focus." He tucked a strand of hair behind her ear. "Nothing can keep me away from you." She was as much a part of him as the heart in his chest.

Bekah nodded. "I'll be here."

He twisted the doorknob but hesitated. "Listen, Bekah, whatever happens, I want you to know…"

She closed the distance between them in two strides and took his mouth in a kiss. He gripped the back of her neck, holding her close and drinking her in like it was their last. Her magic tingled on his lips, but if she felt his emotions—if she had any clue what he was planning—she didn't let on.

Resting her hands on his chest, she looked into his eyes. "I know. I do too."

He nodded and stepped onto the porch, closing the door between them.

CHAPTER ELEVEN

BEKAH PACED IN FRONT OF THE DOOR, WRINGING her hands and cursing herself for not giving Shane her phone. He'd been gone three hours, and Chase was due to pick him up in twenty minutes to head out to the swamp.

"How long does it take to clear your mind?" He didn't run away. He promised he'd be back.

Maybe he'd lost track of time, but the sinking sun should have clued him in that night would fall soon. After three hours, he could be anywhere in the city. He could be lost or hurt. Maybe the return of his memory had been temporary. If confusion set in and he was miles away from home, there was no telling where he could have gone.

She stepped onto the front porch and peered

down the road, but there was no sign of Shane. In a few more minutes, the sun would dip behind the buildings, and the pinks and blues of the sky would morph to deep purples and reds.

She started down the steps, but her ringtone sounded from inside the house, and she darted to the kitchen, whisking her phone from the table. "Hello?"

"Where is Shane?" The wariness in Rain's voice made her stomach drop.

"I don't know. He went for a walk, and he hasn't come back. Is Chase on his way?"

"I'm with Rain," Chase said into the phone.

"You need to come to the bakery now. I just got a call from the high priestess. A werewolf stopped by the coven looking for an amnesia spell. He didn't have any money, so he traded a saxophone for the potion."

"He didn't." She picked up her purse and headed out the door before she realized her feet were moving.

"He did." Irritation edged her brother's voice. "The witches didn't recognize him, so they reported it to Rain. They're going to return the sax, but dammit, Bekah. If he—"

"Thank the goddess the coven is trying to get along with the pack or we may have never known," Rain said. "How fast can you get here?"

"I'm on my way."

When Bekah entered the bakery, Chase locked the door and ushered her to the kitchen. Rain had filled a large copper bowl with water and set it on the counter, where she peered into it, whispering a rhyming verse.

"She put a locator spell on the bracelet you gave him, and she's trying to find it." Chase crossed his arms. "Does he think he can just forget any of this ever happened and the threat will cease to exist? That's not how demons work."

"Found him." Rain sprinkled an herb into the bowl and stirred it with her finger. "He's in the nature preserve to the west."

Chase growled. "What the hell is he doing out there?"

Bekah's stomach turned. "He's going to fight it on his own. The potion was to erase me from his memory in case the demon wins."

She leaned against the counter and tipped her head back. How could she have been so stupid? She'd felt it in him. His apprehension, determination along with a sickening feeling of imminent doom. She'd chalked the emotions up to nerves. Hell, she'd be scared to death if she had to fight a demon, even with the help of four of the pack's strongest wolves.

She'd tried to give him space to work it out, when

she should have called bullshit the moment he picked up his saxophone. "I should have known he'd do this."

"You're an empath, not a clairvoyant. And look…" Rain wrapped her arm around Bekah's shoulders and held up a vial of pink powder. "I made a remedy, but…"

"I don't like the sound of that but."

"The witch he found is powerful, but she's an idiot. She's been known to…" She closed her eyes and shook her head. "She botched the spell."

Nausea churned in her stomach. "What are you trying to say?"

"She didn't cast an amnesia spell. I had her explain what she did, and he'll lose his memories like he asked…but if we don't get to him in time, he'll lose his ability to think at all." She sucked in a deep breath and blew it out hard. "She cast a mind deterioration spell. He'll lose everything: his memories, his personality, his ability to make decisions. It could be permanent."

Rain's words crashed into her like a tidal wave, hollowing out her chest. "How could…? Why…?"

"I don't know. Those spells are forbidden, and the high priestess herself is taking care of the witch who cast it. But Bekah…if his memory has completely faded when we find him, this remedy won't bring it back. All it will do is stop the deterioration. What's gone will be gone for good."

She tried to swallow, but her throat had formed into a knot. "So, he may never remember me?"

"He might not."

"Either way, we need to get to him before the demon does, or his memories won't matter. Let's go." Chase gestured toward the door, and they followed him outside, piling into Rain's car.

Bekah's fear tipped toward panic as she buckled her seatbelt and closed her eyes, her quick, shallow breaths making her head spin. Letting the demon get to him wasn't an option. Her soul was bound to Shane's, and losing him would tear her life apart.

"It's barely dark. We'll get there in time." Rain flashed a small smile as she peered over the back of the seat.

"What if we don't?" The words felt like sandpaper on her throat.

"He's got a powerful aura. Have some faith."

Chase grunted into his phone. "Yeah. See you there." He glanced at her in the rearview mirror. "Luke and the others are on their way. You two stay in the car until the demon is vanquished."

Bekah glared at him. "I'm not afraid of a demon."

He clenched his teeth. "You're defenseless."

Rain put her hand on his knee. "We'll be fine, dear. I'll strike it with a bolt of lightning if it gets anywhere near her."

He blew out a hard breath and took Rain's hand. "Both of you be careful, please."

As the sun sank behind the horizon, Shane followed a trail deeper into the woods. Spanish moss hung like drapes from cypress trees, creating a canopy over the path and making the hiking trail appear more like a tunnel into the ominous night.

The dirt path veered left, so Shane went right, twigs and dry leaves crunching beneath his boots as he ventured farther into the swamp. As he neared the water, the ground turned soft, the mud clinging to his shoes and making a sucking sound with each step he took.

"This is far enough away from civilization, I guess." He found a dry patch of ground and leaned against a tree, uncapping the potion bottle he'd gotten from the witch. The sickly-sweet cotton candy scent singed his nostrils, and nausea churned in his gut.

Leaning his head back against the tree trunk, he

closed his eyes and offered a prayer to whatever god might be listening. "If I make it through this, please help me find my way back to Bekah."

He tossed back the potion like a shot of whiskey, cringing as the syrupy liquid coated his throat, burning its way down to his stomach. His pulse thrummed as he shoved the empty bottle into his pocket. A spinning sensation in his head forced his eyes shut, and he gripped the tree to steady himself.

An image of Bekah formed behind his lids, her hazel eyes crinkling with her sexy smile, but he forced it from his mind. She was the first thing he needed to forget.

"I'm here you wanker, come and get me." With his blood link to the demon, it wouldn't take the bastard long to find him.

Pushing from the trunk, he stumbled forward, his vision blurring for a moment before coming into focus. The scents of mud, cypress, and decaying foliage filled his senses, and he blinked, taking in his surroundings.

Why was he in the swamp?

If he'd come to hunt, he'd have shifted by now. He spun in a circle, trying to get his bearings, wracking his brain for the reason he'd come here, but his mind felt like a void. Confusion pinched his brow, and a flush of icy panic raced through his veins.

He couldn't remember anything.

A rustling in the brush drew his attention, and the putrid scent of rancid garbage assaulted his senses before the creature stepped into view. Standing nearly seven feet tall, the demon had slick, maroon skin and a set of short, wicked-sharp horns atop its head. One hundred pointed teeth filled its lipless maw, and elongated fingers curled into talons that could gut a werewolf with one swipe.

The demon snarled, and Shane's wolf took over, his body vibrating as it transformed into his beast. Crouching low, he backpedaled, the ridge of hair on his back standing on end as he assessed the fiend for a weak spot.

A vein pulsed on the monster's neck, and Shane locked his focus on the heartbeat, peeling his lips back in a growl. He shifted onto his haunches and sprang.

As his teeth latched onto the demon's neck, it spun, flinging him into a tree. The impact cracked the thin trunk, forcing the breath from Shane's lungs, and he hit the ground with a smack. The sharp, coppery taste of demon blood filled his mouth, and the thick, black-red substance trailed down the fiend's shoulder.

Grunting, Shane scrambled to his feet and lunged again, latching onto the monster's leg and dragging it to the ground. The fiend wailed and gripped him by the scruff of his neck like a pup, tossing him aside as if he were merely a mild inconvenience.

Shane rolled through the leaves, his nails gripping the dirt as he righted himself, adrenaline pooling in his muscles as he sprang toward the demon again.

The fiend caught him by the throat and lifted him into the air.

His legs flailing, Shane rotated his torso, trying to break from the demon's clutches. It merely tightened its grip on his throat. Shane gasped for breath that wouldn't come. Darkness tunneled his vision.

Turning its free hand palm up, the demon reached a claw toward Shane's nostril. The sharp tip burrowed into his snout, and fiery heat consumed his head, his senses thickening until they ceased to register anything but the pain. Intense pressure pushed on his skull from the inside out as the inferno of his brain threatened to explode.

Thunder clapped from above, and an electric jolt zipped through his body as he crashed to the ground. He sucked a ragged breath into his starving lungs and lifted his head. The world spun, and he lay his head in the dirt, giving himself time to heal from the attack.

His senses returning, the snarling, grunting sounds of a battle registered in his ears. A female shouted, "Shane!" and he stumbled to his paws to find a pack of werewolves fighting the demon.

A chocolate-colored wolf lunged toward it, clamping onto its arm before it tossed him aside. A gray wolf went for its chest, but it knocked him aside before he could make contact. The alpha of the pack, an enormous light-brown wolf, attacked, gripping the demon's injured neck and dragging it to the ground.

Shane growled. This was his demon. He couldn't recall why, but he was connected to this atrocity, and it was his duty to vanquish it.

The wolves continued attacking, the demon deflecting their advances as it moved toward Shane. He stalked forward and joined the fray, sinking his teeth into leathery flesh before being knocked to the ground.

The alpha howled, and his pack responded, lunging in unison, four maws clamping onto the demon's soft spots from behind. Shane growled and leaped toward it, swiping his claws across the fiend's chest, piercing its heart.

It exploded into a cloud of ash, leaving Shane face-to-face with a pack of angry werewolves.

Bekah hid behind the bushes, Rain's fingers digging into her arm the only thing keeping her from running into the middle of the standoff. Through the bramble, she glimpsed the deep-brown fur standing in a ridge down Shane's back. His eyes were wild, his posture defensive as Luke and the others fanned out around him in a semicircle.

"He's scared." She tugged from Rain's grip. "He doesn't recognize them. They're making it worse."

Bekah darted into the clearing behind Shane. "You need to shift, Luke. He feels threatened."

Shane snapped his head around at the sound of her voice and snarled.

Her stomach plummeted to her feet as she scrambled backward into a tree. "It's me, Shane. It's Bekah." She slipped a trembling hand into her pocket, closing her fingers around the vial of powder.

Shane turned back to the wolves, a defensive growl rumbling in his throat.

Luke's nostrils flared as he blew out a hard breath and jerked his head upward. His body shimmered, his human form taking shape as he stood on two feet. Chase and the others followed his lead, shifting and moving closer to the alpha.

The tension in Shane's haunches loosened, but he hesitated to shift.

"We're not going to hurt you, buddy." Luke raised his hands. "We just want to talk."

As Luke moved toward him, Shane took two cautious steps back, his lips peeling back to bare his teeth.

Her muscles trembling, Bekah crept toward Shane, one arm outstretched, her other hand gripping the possible remedy for his amnesia. He glanced between Luke and her, blinking and tilting his head as she finally held his gaze.

"You know me, Shane." She reached for him, running her hand along the soft fur of his neck. Opening her senses to him, she felt his confusion and fear. He was lost and on the verge of bolting. "Please shift so we can talk. I want to help you."

Rain shuffled to her side. "He needs to be in human form for the spell to work...*if* it's going to work."

"Please, Shane." She leaned in, her face dangerously close to his razor-sharp teeth, and Chase let out a disapproving grunt.

Slowly, she drifted closer, pressing her lips to his forehead and clutching his fur as tears gathered on her lower lids. She was his fate-bound, damn it. She shouldn't be so easily erased from his mind. A sob bubbled up from her chest, and she released him, allowing the tears to drip onto her cheeks. His wolf should have recognized her.

If this remedy didn't work… If the amnesia was permanent this time, she might have to spend the rest of her life bound to a man who wasn't bound to her. Shane had stolen her heart the day she met him, and it had been beating inside him ever since. She couldn't lose him.

"You know me." She clenched her teeth, fisting her hands at her sides. "Damn it, Shane, your wolf knows me. *Remember.*"

He stepped back, his gaze darting between Bekah and her packmates as a deep whimper emanated from his throat. Locking eyes with her, he sucked in a deep breath and shifted to his human form.

His brow furrowed over his sea-green eyes, and he took two cautious steps toward her. "Where are we?"

She swallowed the baseball-sized lump from her throat. "The Louisiana swamp, near New Orleans."

He blinked, his face scrunching like it did before when he couldn't access a memory. "How did I get here?"

Her heart sank, and she cursed the witch who gave him a botched spell. The woman's stupidity had wrenched Bekah's soulmate from her grasp, tearing a gaping hole in her heart. Spending the rest of her life in love with a man who couldn't remember he loved her back was unimaginable.

She dumped the remedy powder into her palm. He may not remember her, but at least Rain's spell would stop him from losing any more of himself. "You walked here to fight a demon. You were trying to protect me."

He met her gaze, and a look of recognition smoothed his features. "I know you, don't I?"

Her blood felt fizzy, hope blooming in her heart as she moved toward him. "You do know me."

"You... Are we...?" He squeezed his eyes shut and shook his head. "Why do I get the feeling I'm in love with you?"

"Because you are." She blew the remedy into his face, and he coughed, fanning it away. "And I'm in love with you too."

As the cloud of shimmering powder dissipated, Shane smiled. Pink crystals clung to his lashes, drifting onto his cheeks as he blinked.

Sweet relief flushed her system as she returned the smile. Even if his other memories never returned, their soul-deep connection remained intact. He may have lost his past, but his future was here with her. "Do you remember me?"

He stepped toward her, placing a hand on her hip and cupping her face in his other, running his thumb over her cheek. "You're my fate-bound, Bekah. I could never forget you." He brushed his lips to hers. "Well, not for long anyway."

EPILOGUE

SHANE STOOD IN THE WING, WATCHING HIS student finish his piano solo. As the audience clapped, the boy stood and bowed, and Shane strode onto the stage.

He shook the kid's hand and addressed the audience. "Let's hear another round for Jacob. Wasn't he brilliant?"

The little boy beamed with pride and hurried down the steps to his mother's waiting arms.

"Last up is Emma on saxophone." He motioned for her to join him on stage, and his heart swelled with love as she shuffled toward him. His old sax was nearly as big as her, and she cradled it to her chest as she turned toward the audience.

"Knock 'em dead, sweetheart." He kissed the top

of her head and descended the steps to join Bekah in the front row.

His music school had been in business for six months, and though he only had fifteen students performing, their first recital had drawn a crowd. Half the pack had shown up, filling the small auditorium to the brim, and the kids were thrilled to be playing for more than their own parents.

Emma played her version of "You are my Sunshine," and he slipped his hand into Bekah's. "She's good."

Bekah rested her head on his shoulder. "She has a good teacher."

She finished the song, and the pack rose to their feet, giving her a standing ovation. Emma's smile lit up the room, and he joined her on the stage to wrap up the show.

As the parents left with their kids, the pack hung around, congratulating Emma and shaking Shane's hand one by one, showing their support. His throat tightened as the alpha clapped him on the shoulder and told him he did a great job. Moving to New Orleans, being with Bekah, and joining the pack was the best decision he'd ever made.

For the first time in his life, he belonged somewhere. Being a part of a pack...part of a family...was everything he'd ever wanted. And the beautiful woman standing before him had made that happen.

The botched spell the witch gave him had clouded his memories, which turned out to be a blessing. It had been easy to dismiss his preconceived notions about pack life when he could hardly remember the reason he'd avoided it before. While his past wasn't as sharp in his mind as it used to be, his future couldn't have been any clearer.

The pack finally dispersed, leaving him alone with his new family. Emma put his sax in the case and carried it onto the stage.

She hugged her mom. "You said if I practiced hard and stuck with it, I could get my own saxophone."

"I sure did, didn't I?"

Shane knelt beside Emma and put his hand on the case. The worn leather was smooth against his skin, and the memories attached to the instrument—happy memories he could still recall—would live on in his heart. "You know what, Emma? You can have mine."

She looked at him with wide eyes. "But your mom gave it to you."

"And now, I'm giving it to you."

Emma hugged his neck. "Thank you."

He held her in his arms and blinked back the pressure forming in his eyes. "I have a present for your mum too. The one we talked about before. Do you think she's ready for it?"

She giggled and grabbed Bekah's hand tugging her toward him. "I know she is."

With one knee on the ground, Shane pulled a diamond ring from his pocket. "Bekah, I know you wanted to hold off on becoming mates, so Emma could get used to me...but she assures me she's ready."

He glanced at Emma, and she giggled again. "She's been pestering me to do this for months, in fact. So..." He took Bekah's hand. "Will you be my mate...my wife?"

A single tear spilled from Bekah's eye as she pulled him to his feet. "You two discussed this without me?"

"Someone had to make you stop dragging your feet, Mom. We're all ready." Emma opened the saxophone case and ran her hand over the brass. "Well, go on and say yes."

Bekah smiled and took his face in her hands. "Yes, Shane. I love you." Her eyes glistened, and as she smiled, another tear rolled down her cheek.

He kissed it away. "I love you too, Bekah. Thank you for making all my dreams come true."

Emma tugged on his shirt. "Can I start calling you Dad now, or do I have to wait until after the ceremony?"

He laughed and scooped her up with one arm, holding Bekah tight against his side with the other. "You can call me Dad whenever you want."

Emma put an arm around his neck, the other around her mom's. "It's about time. I told you that you can't fight fate, remember?"

He kissed them both. "How could I forget?"

ALSO BY CARRIE PULKINEN

Fire Witches of Salem Series

Chaos and Ash

Commanding Chaos

Claiming Chaos

New Orleans Nocturnes Series

License to Bite

Shift Happens

Life's a Witch

Santa Got Run Over by a Vampire

Finders Reapers

Swipe Right to Bite

Batshift Crazy

Collection One: Books 1-3

Collection Two: Books 4 - 7

Crescent City Wolf Pack Series

Werewolves Only

Beneath a Blue Moon

Bound by Blood

A Deal with Death

A Song to Remember

Shifting Fate

Collection One: Books 1-3

Collection Two: Books 4-6

Haunted Ever After Series

Love at First Haunt

Second Chance Spirit

Third Time's a Ghost

Love and Ghosts

Love and Omens

Love and Curses

Collection One: Books 1 - 3

Collection Two: Books 4 - 6

Stand Alone Books

Flipping the Bird

Sign Steal Deliver

Azrael

Lilith

The Rest of Forever

Soul Catchers

Bewitching the Vampire

ABOUT THE AUTHOR

Carrie Pulkinen is a paranormal romance author who has always been fascinated with things that go bump in the night. Of course, when you grow up next door to a cemetery, the dead (and the undead) are hard to ignore. Pair that with her passion for writing and her love of a good happily-ever-after, and becoming a paranormal romance author seems like the only logical career choice.

Before she decided to turn her love of the written word into a career, Carrie spent the first part of her professional life as a high school journalism and yearbook teacher. She loves good chocolate and bad puns, and in her free time, she likes to read, drink wine, and travel with her family.

Connect with Carrie online:
www.CarriePulkinen.com

Made in the USA
Columbia, SC
02 January 2024

29717071R10102